Claudia

Misguided Spirit

A MEMOIR

Pamela Hendricks Frautschi

CLAUDIA
MISGUIDED SPIRIT

iUniverse books may be ordered through booksellers or by contacting:

iUniverse
1663 Liberty Drive
Bloomington, IN 47403
www.iuniverse.com
1-800-Authors (1-800-288-4677)

Because of the dynamic nature of the Internet, any web addresses or links contained in this book may have changed since publication and may no longer be valid. The views expressed in this work are solely those of the author and do not necessarily reflect the views of the publisher, and the publisher hereby disclaims any responsibility for them.

ISBN: 978-1-4917-4875-6 (sc)
ISBN: 978-1-4917-4874-9 (e)

Library of Congress Control Number: 2014918708

Printed in the United States of America.

iUniverse rev. date: 11/17/2014

Dedication

For all the family and friends whose suggestions helped, and for those who were along for this whale of a ride.

Acknowledgements

Special thanks to Linda Dunakin whose knowledge and skills provided excellent guidance, and whose half-century of continuing friendship is cherished.

For the book's appropriate sub-title, special thanks to Richard Ippolito.

Author's Note

This book is a reflection with focus on my relationship with my sister "Claudia" for over half a century. Names of all the characters have been changed to provide some cushion of privacy and anonymity to those involved. Writing the book helped bring understanding and closure for the damages done in the challenging course of this relationship. It may help bring catharsis to readers who share parallel experiences within their families.

Putting pen to paper is a regular practice for me, a way to clarify my feelings, to sort out conflicts that weigh on my mind, to capture memories, to evaluate solutions. I recall doing so as early as age seven. At that time I wrote what I considered to be a scathing objection to a childhood friend's mother regarding the damages her parenting was doing to her daughter. I didn't deliver my letter. I knew that I, a child, wasn't entitled to do that. But I sure felt good about writing it. Worried, however, about its being discovered, I took it and a packet of matches to my backyard. As the letter burned and its ashes drifted in the wind, I figured that the essence of my message would magically and anonymously spread through the air to my friend's mother. I felt satisfied.

Much of my writing is just for me. Some is intended to be shared. Friends with whom I've shared various writings and reports over the years have repeatedly said, "You should publish." I never took the time to pursue it because life is full of exhilarating people and activities to enjoy alongside simply keeping up with responsibilities.

Knowing that I'd been writing about the episodes and impacts of my sister, and experiencing seventeen years of them himself, my husband not only said, "You should publish," but he put a publisher in touch with me. Hence, <u>Claudia, Misguided Spirit</u> evolved. She is distinctive, but also is a familiar character in many families.

It's my hope that families that have a "Claudia" member, can benefit from my experiences, and move on more quickly and comfortably than I did. I also hope that readers who are the "Claudias" of their own families can benefit from this outside view of themselves even if they need to burn the book to magically receive the message. Those readers who aren't Claudias, and are in families exempt from such characters, can take the ride vicariously and feel lucky.

Table of Contents

Chapters

Spirit/Background/Rebellion

Claudia became the Captain Ahab in my family. We didn't foresee that outcome. Our family, with intentions of complementing a pleasing and fulfilling life, had strongly valued and supported her talents, intelligence and promising potential. Claudia was demanding, purposeful and daring, elements that require discipline but can be admired in a child, and are customary in a teenager. But as an adult, like Ahab, Claudia was driven without regard for the damages she would do to herself and the rest of us in the process. For an artist and poet, five-foot one-inch female of fluid demeanor and masterful manipulative skills, Claudia took us for a whale of a ride.

In her mid-thirties Claudia proclaimed to me that she was a Spirit, and as such was placed in our family as her punishment to work off bad karma from her past lives. With commanding seriousness Claudia went on to say that her objective was to have a life of joy, beauty and love in order to reach Nirvana. She believed that achievement would finally exempt her from the misfortunes of human existence.

I, nine years younger, and the last of the four children in our six-member family, found her karmic viewpoint intriguing. My earliest experiences of Claudia, memories from the time I was age two onward, were that Claudia was in a different league from the rest of us. Claudia's league was superior. Claudia's attitude toward me and those who weren't members of the superior league was one of disdain. Her proclamation and focus on being a Spirit perhaps explained why she had regarded all my youthful adventures and misadventures as personal aggravations and obstacles in her life. Her karmic viewpoint, diminishing, if not erasing the value of bloodline and family allegiance, made my life and all others only footnotes to hers, disdainful ones at that. I didn't take solace in the message. Maintaining at least a vestige of family with Claudia was important to me. My efforts in that regard tided me through many challenging experiences with her.

Claudia's disclosures about her spiritual placement in our family, and her mission of joy, beauty and love on the path to Nirvana, were fascinating. But even without them, Claudia was a fascinating creature who lived a fascinating life. Claudia's mission also exposed the folly of my longing for a sisterly relationship with her. That sisterly, or sisterly-brotherly relationship I felt existed with my other siblings, would be an outrageous pursuit with a Spirit. I preferred communication on a human level.

During our adult lives on occasions when Claudia sensed that I was being far too human with her, she tried to elicit the Spirit in me. That proved to be a frustrating and disconcerting experience for both of our Spirits. Clearly my Spirit was a lowly one by comparison, provoking Claudia to scream at me, "Come up! Come up!" The screaming simply frightened my inferior Spirit away, and unfortunately tapped into the vexations of my human nature.

Claudia held to the belief that she was on a spiritual quest. She titled her first collection of self-published poetry "The Quest." Its thirty or more poems were written after she'd determined and explored elements of her Spirit/Mission. Its poetry reflected upon many of her favorite places and travels: Mt Everest, India, the Taj Mahal, safari lands of Africa, Paris, Cape Cod, Colorado, California's Pacific coast, sights and experiences that "answered the song of my soul." She considered realism an evasion, reality a lie, disrupting the pursuits of spiritual dreams.

During those travels Claudia had not contacted me. To her I probably remained among her "annoying child and teenager" memories, not worth thinking about, the bottom of her footnote's list. Not being with Claudia, or knowing of her "Spirit/Mission" for such a long period, I was surprised by a call and request from her. She planned to visit me in my new home in Milwaukee. The purpose of her trip wasn't just to see me and meet my husband of four years. The purpose was to bring Jouster, her poodle, from her home in California to stay with us for the year she was on sabbatical from her teaching position. Her sabbatical period was to be devoted to filming and photographing the museums and famous works of art in Europe and Egypt.

Besides being an artist and poet, she was an accomplished photographer. Clever and enterprising, she'd convinced the school system to foot the bill in exchange for a remarkable film and photograph product that would enhance their system. Her only problem was that she couldn't take Jouster, the poodle, with her, nor bear to kennel him. Finding a loving home for her dog in Milwaukee was an important mission accomplished.

I invited our parents in northern Indiana to join us. They too hadn't seen Claudia for about five years. I couldn't imagine excluding them from this reunion. They were to pick her up at O'Hare and stay for the few days she'd be with us, and then drop her off at O'Hare on their way home.

They all arrived as scheduled. Claudia educated us on Jouster's habits and demonstrated all his cute tricks. The three days passed relatively smoothly but not entirely without incident. Perhaps Claudia's strongest moment of displeasure was when my husband stated that it was fine that Jouster slept with her, but that Jouster would not be sleeping in our bed. Concluding that she had no better option for Jouster, Jouster stayed, and Claudia went off on a year's adventure.

We soon learned that Jouster's two favorite places to pee while we were away at work were our new loveseat in the living room, and our expensive new king-sized bedspread. Over time we devised various containment policies to spare our loveseat and bedspread from Jouster's habits. We also adjusted to his preferences for people-food and his repugnance for dog food.

Jouster adjusted reluctantly to our purchasing a leash and walking him around the block morning and evening. But when Wisconsin's winter snows arrived, Jouster balked so strongly at walks that he renewed and strengthened his attraction to the loveseat and the bedspread. We had the "Dry Clean Only" bedspread cleaned several times, and hired a professional service to clean and deodorize the loveseat. At that time in our lives, such expenses meant sacrifices in other areas. Jouster unfortunately couldn't counterbalance these episodes with new methods of endearing himself to us.

When Claudia returned from her year-long sabbatical, my folks once again provided transport from O'Hare. All of us were eager to hear reports of Claudia's trip, especially since she'd sent no communications along the way. Jouster too was very excited to see her. Claudia's initial reunion with us was subdued, mainly conveying that she was exhausted and constipated. However, she responded with lots of cuddles and enthusiastic animation to Jouster who gave her the lappy-licky kisses of which we had not grown fond. When she finally put Jouster down, he made a beeline to the loveseat and lifted his leg.

Tom leapt out of his chair and loudly shouted, "No, No, No!" He scooped up Jouster with pee trailing on the floor, rushed out the front door and unceremoniously dropped the dog on the front yard. Claudia leapt up too, thunderstruck by what had just occurred. With full fury, she lambasted Tom for his severe mistreatment of poor little Jouster.

As shocked as Tom was at Claudia's outburst, he made some calm and simple statement like, "The dog can't be allowed to pee in the house."

Claudia retrieved her cowering, trembling, empty-bladder dog, and retreated to her room as she mumbled sympathies to Jouster.

For the next two days Claudia was in foul humor. Each time she could corner me when no one else was around she had a steady stream of criticism coming my way. Who was that man I'd married? How could I abide someone who was so cruel to animals? Why did I have to include Mother and Dad again for the brief time we had together, since she couldn't stand to be around Mother? How could I stand the syrupy sweetness of Mother and the old stories she repeated? Why had I let my hair grow so long? Why didn't I pluck my eyebrows and make some efforts to improve my appearance? Why did I wear clothes that were orange and so unbecoming to me? Why had I not run out to buy her some Ex-Lax when she told me she was constipated?

Then, in the midst of her statements about how she just didn't understand people, people who were cruel to animals, people who thought their repeated stories were cute and entertaining, people who rejected looking as good as they easily could, is when she told me that she was a Spirit and had a mission of joy, beauty and love.

People I told of that scenario reflected on parallels with their relatives or with difficult dogs. It's probably no surprise that I was relieved when Claudia and Jouster flew back to California. In a phone call with my folks the next day, though Dad rarely spoke on the phone, he thanked me for the good meals, said the house was shaping up nicely, and not to worry myself about Claudia. I appreciated his saying, "She has some high falootin' ideas. The main problem with her dog is that she thinks it's human."

Dad was a no-nonsense, tough kind of guy. Dad was a sponge of a reader and a controversial thinker. He was raised on an Illinois farm, believed in education, got his Master's Degree from the University of Chicago and was a high school geography teacher. He read magazines, classic epics, novels and paperbacks prolifically. He was a drinking, smoking, swearing, hunting, fishing and fix-everything man. His objectionable habits were the antithesis of my mother, but she also was a teacher and could sew, upholster and fix nearly everything as well.

When their first daughter, Elli, arrived, she was the apple of Dad's eye. Four years later, along came large-eyed, pug-nosed, Claudia, regularly attired in adorable outfits that Mother made for her. In her cute and clever toddlerhood she became everybody's favorite for the next seven years until the one and only boy in the family, Brett, was born. Everyone was thrilled to have a boy in the family. I arrived two years later, probably intended to be Brett's little brother, a job I did pretty well.

In short, we were two sets of children in one family: the pair of big sisters and the little kids. My memories are that Claudia and Elli never got along and that Claudia adored Brett to the exclusion of me. To me Elli was a kind and caring substitute mother especially when Claudia was frolicking and having fun with Brett.

Claudia and Elli were both excellent academic achievers and both were quite pretty despite their different body types, facial features and hair styles. Claudia was more petite and graceful in movement, and her large gorgeous aquamarine eyes distinguished her from all of us. Claudia was more instantly popular in high school, and Elli had to lick her wounds stoically when Claudia was invited into the most elite social club of girls. Such clubs constituted an important part of life during high school years in that era.

Claudia grew moody in her teens, without reserve expressing her displeasures as much as her joys. When she was assigned to my father's geography class, she was furious, especially after he corrected an answer she'd given in class in front of her peers. She never forgave him for that humiliation despite her lifelong admiration of his knowledge and cognitive abilities.

Although Mother had admirable social skills and a fine sense of fashion, always making beautiful clothes, costumes and prom dresses for her daughters, in Claudia's opinion that didn't stand up to the material wealth and opportunities of her friends. Yearnings for higher economic status were perhaps the only ideas she and Elli held in common.

The situation that infuriated Claudia most was that she had to work and live at home for a year after high school graduation because our folks couldn't afford to have two kids in college at the same time. Elli finished her senior year of college while Claudia wallowed in the chagrin of being a working girl at her far-from-glamorous job at Standard Equipment, working among sinks and toilets and light fixtures when she knew she was destined to become a great artist.

Claudia had many natural talents. When she was little, Mother sent her to dancing school. Claudia loved it and loved her male dancing instructor. She always stole the show at recitals. At that time Claudia thought she'd become a famous dancer, unique, and world-renowned. The instructor's suicide put an end to Claudia's dance lessons. Her art talent moved forward. Our high school's exotic art teacher noticed Claudia's special skills. The teacher's influence motivated Claudia to follow the joy and beauty of art. Her class went on a field trip to the Art Institute of Chicago, which would prove to be another turning point in her life.

Knowing that Claudia had loved the Art Institute trip, a girlfriend invited Claudia to take the train with her to Chicago. Claudia could continue looking at art while the friend attended an appointment. Upon entering the museum Claudia's friend noticed that art classes were being offered to high school students during the summer. She suggested that she and Claudia sign up. Claudia protested that she couldn't afford it even though there was nothing that she'd love more. So her friend marched into the Institute's Administrative Offices and talked them into letting the girls do odd jobs to defray half the cost of classes. Claudia's friend obtained all the necessary information and arranged a date for them to begin.

Claudia knew that Dad wouldn't spend a penny for such art classes. Claudia would simply find ways to convince Mother to give her money from occasional cash Mother squirreled away. Whatever reasons or motivations Mother had, and whatever frays Mother had with Dad about it, Mother gave Claudia the money.

Claudia took the classes at the Art Institute. She also addressed, stamped and sealed many invitations along with doing a variety of other tasks. Whenever she found a time-gap between jobs and classes, she studied every gallery area and artwork in the Institute. She said she would stand before these great works of art with her heart pounding wildly in her chest. She'd feel short of breath she was so awed and entranced by these works of art. At one point while in a gallery by herself she was so overwhelmed that she thought she was going to faint. So she walked over to the wall, backed against it, and slid to the floor. Then she felt terrified that the guard would walk by and find her.

I asked why she was terrified, since telling the guard of faintness would bring help. Claudia however told me that she would feel unforgivably embarrassed, and she thought she'd be in trouble. That was because she suspected that she wasn't supposed to be in a gallery by herself. She was fearful that the Institute would tell her parents. That too puzzled me. Maybe Dad never knew about the Art Institute classes.

After the year Claudia unhappily endured at Standard Equipment, Elli graduated from college and came home. On this rare occasion when all of us were together Mother had a friend come over to take our family photograph. In the picture, all of us are looking at the camera and smiling, except Claudia. She didn't want her picture taken. She had protested multiple times until she was at least talked into sitting on the couch with us. There she was with her arms folded across her chest, her eyes cast down, and a very sour expression on her face. It was a picture Claudia hated. For me, the picture was exactly the way things were.

For Claudia, later with her formulated karmic thesis, the photograph constituted a classic reminder of the misfortune her Spirit endured by being in such an insistent and manipulative family. But before she became an aficionado of Eastern religions and defined the elements constituting who and what she was, the photograph depicted Claudia as an exasperated teenager who, as many teenagers feel, had suffered the glitch of being born into the wrong family. Claudia, despite her exasperations, was sustained in a loving, intelligent, functional family. She certainly wasn't raised with Ozzie and Harriet parents, but she was raised in an environment where she was valued, encouraged, protected and had comfortable provisions.

Claudia and Elli later said that at some point in their childhood Mother had a miscarriage and suffered a breakdown. What caused it and how long it lasted were never described, nor was it likely that it was ever professionally diagnosed and Mother was not institutionalized.

Perhaps it was during that period that my sisters became critical of Mother and felt so entitled to their resentments later in life.

Mother was raised as a Christian Scientist. Dad had no interest in having his wife practice Christian Science or having his children raised as such. Mother's withdrawal from the Christian Science practices caused her problems with her own mother and occasionally with her siblings.

Mother also lost her teaching job after she and Dad were married. Mom and Dad kept their marriage secret and lived apart for the first year so that she could keep her job a while longer. In those days married women had to stop teaching. Schools didn't want their students exposed to the possibility of pregnant women as role models. Female teachers were spinsters or widows. Mother had loved teaching and working with students. When she and Dad started living together, the loss of her teaching job and its associated friends was a big change for her.

Financial pressures on this young family, including our maternal grandmother's expectation of financial assistance from her children, may have brought the breaking point. Gramma, widowed and left without means when the youngest of her five children was still an infant, managed the family by running a rooming house. When Mother had stopped working and sending part of her money to Gramma, a portion of Dad's earnings was sent. Needing his full salary for his own family, Dad put a stop to that when Claudia was born.

Despite Dad's manly rough edges, he was a true half of the parenting team. He sang us little songs he'd made up, read to us at bedtime, played board games and cards with us, and did half of the cooking. He was not a proponent of organized religion, finding too much about it hypocritical or destructive. But Mom directed the nursery school at church. She particularly enjoyed pre-school and kindergarten children and all the crafts, songs and games to play with them. Mother was always a community activist as well, writing a regular column as a proponent of war bonds during WWII. She also did book review programs for women's clubs and was on the Board of Directors of the orphanage. Performing in Civic Little Theatre productions was another thing she loved and did regularly. She was quite like Helen Hayes. In later years Mom's white hair pulled up in a bun, her colorful voice, animated gestures and engaging demeanor were well-suited to the roles that made Helen famous. As Elli and Claudia grew older they speculated on what a successful stage or screen career Mother might have had if she hadn't had a family. Perhaps all of Mother's natural talents and relentless energy intimidated both girls and Dad. She was a tough act to follow.

Mother told endearing stories about Claudia, a precocious child, cute, quick, imaginative and creative as a preschooler. Enchanted by her adorable little daughter Claudia, Mother remembered and recited the spontaneous little poems Claudia made up and would recite to other children. Mother talked about the miniature dollhouse she created for her two elder daughters and the funny conversations and situations she'd overhear Claudia chattering about between the characters and the pets in the dollhouse. And Claudia certainly looked adorable in the ensembles Mother made for her in those early years.

The uncooperative, often disdainful relationship Claudia had with Elli was well established long before Brett and I came on the scene. Elli was more invested in being a good girl who would make her parents proud. Claudia was more rebellious and daring. For instance in high school when she discovered e. e. cummings, Claudia wrote all her term papers in lower case as he did. If she was marked down for lack of capitalization, she'd make a point about e. e. cummings as a poet of merit certainly worthy of emulation.

Claudia, much later, past her own mid-life, told me that Mother had told her that since Dad was adoring of toddler Elli, and treated Elli as "his child," Mother decided to have a child of her own. That second child was Claudia. Claudia felt she was treated as Mother's "possession". In that regard Claudia felt Mother always drew attention to her with expectations that Claudia would "perform" to show how remarkable, exceptional, and adorable "Mother's child" was. This perhaps was the source of Claudia's perpetual need to be in the center ring throughout her life.

*　*　*　*　*

Claudia finally escaped home by going to college at Indiana University. Disappointed in the sorority she'd pledged, and in her Art major there, after a year she transferred to University of Miami-Coral Gables for the remainder of her undergraduate work. She spent the interim summer studying art once again at Chicago's Art Institute, creating diverse and impressive artworks for her portfolio.

Claudia was the first person in our family to book an air flight, her way to Miami. Dressing appropriately for those days, Claudia wore a brand new beige linen suit with matching pumps, white gloves, a small fashionable purse, and carried a beautiful set of beige-colored classic Samsonite luggage.

Brett and I, excited to have our first experience of an airport, were cautioned by Mother not to annoy Claudia on the way. Claudia's plane unfortunately was delayed two hours due to mechanical problems. Finally Mother walked with Claudia outside to the loading stairs. Brett commented about Mom's behavior, brushing her hair wisps away from her face and straightening her clothes as she did the long walk back into the airport.

Brett said, "Look how self-conscious she is and how she thinks that everyone is looking just at her."

Mom's fussy straightening of her hair and her clothes were typical of her. The habit at least made sense in all the winds of the airport. One of Mother's faults was her constant consideration of what other people thought, what their judgments were. It probably never occurred to her how others might sometimes view her as a Nervous Nellie.

Shortly after Claudia's plane took off, Mother looked exceptionally worried. She shushed me to listen to alarming messages on the Public Address system reporting that Claudia's plane had crashed six miles from the airport. The pilot had managed a belly-landing in a farmer's field. Few injuries were reported and they'd be bringing the passengers back to the airport.

Instead of waiting, we drove out to the crash site to see the plane on its belly in the field. Police cars and ambulances were there. Assuming that Claudia was on the passenger bus on its way back to the airport, we too headed back. Claudia was furious in the car as we drove back home because the crash had caused a small hole to be torn in the shoulder of her new linen suit. She was furious because in the initial two-hour delay they hadn't fixed the mechanical problem. Now she was further delayed. In the post-crash hubbub, she'd managed to book herself on the next flight scheduled at midnight to Miami. That provided time to have Mother repair her suit and drive her back to the airport for a flight that went on time and without incident.

We bought a *Chicago Sun Times* newspaper the next day. Its crash report said that three of the four engines dropped out of their encasements as a result of the belly-landing impact. No fatalities occurred. The most serious injury was a broken back. It said that a pert female college student had sustained an arm injury but declined medical attention and took the next flight to Miami.

Adult friends and neighbors were astounded that Claudia, or anyone for that matter, would have the courage to take the next flight out after being in a plane crash. Our grade-school friends thought it was cool that people could even survive a plane crash and cooler still that our sister wasn't going to let a little plane crash keep her from where she was going.

Unlike Mother's "What will the neighbors think?" Claudia wouldn't have cared what any of them thought.

Claudia didn't come home for Thanksgiving, Christmas or any other occasion until the next summer. Then she came home to be Maid of Honor for Elli's June wedding. Claudia's beautiful tan made the rest of us look anemic. More importantly Claudia was smiling and charming with Elli's new cluster of in-laws. In her charming mode Claudia was an animated storyteller and conversationalist. Her stories were peppered with laughter and big-eyed facial expressions that were riveting. Those Caribbean turquoise eyes of hers were magnetic.

*   *   *   *   *

The following summer Claudia came home and went on a week's vacation with us at Gravel Lake in Michigan. This was the first family vacation for Brett and me, so we were particularly enthusiastic about it. Elli and her husband and their first son, already crawling, met us there with a cluster of Elli's in-laws. We stayed in rustic minimalist small log cabins amid the dense pines. Brett and I were intrigued by the realities of wood tics, spring peeper tiny toads, bullfrogs, water spiders and fireplace spiders disguised as stones.

Dad brought all his fishing rods, reels, flies, plugs and equipment. We'd gone fishing with him before, but never in a rowboat or a motorboat. We also loved playing on the pier and swimming to the wooden raft.

Claudia didn't fish. She was totally entertaining with the baby, tickling, singing, making faces and playing with him. Claudia also spent a lot of time by herself, sketching in her sketchbook or reading various books she'd brought along. She did a lot of sleeping and sunbathing on the pier or the raft. And she did a lot of distance swimming. One day she told Brett to row the rowboat across the lake as she swam behind it all the way across that impressive long distance.

Decades later she told me that that was one of the most miserable times of her life. When she swam across Gravel Lake she was hoping not to make it. She thought she was pregnant as a result of a date who had forced himself on her when she'd had too much to drink. Her period was more than a week late when we went on vacation. The day after she swam across Gravel Lake she got her period.

Claudia drank and smoked openly during that vacation. Mother said nothing, but was clearly disappointed. Dad himself probably smoked two packs a day at that time. Mother may have had two experimental cigarettes in her lifetime and she was definitely a teetotaler who disliked alcohol.

Those were the years when Claudia was a party girl with some people who would later become jetsetters. Though Claudia always protested comments that she was sexy, she was sexy. Perhaps she meant that if someone asked her if she'd like to have sex, she'd honestly say no. She probably didn't think of herself as promiscuous, nor take ownership of drinking as a path to promiscuity. Sexiness, drunkenness and promiscuity fit into most chapters of Claudia's life, despite her exceptional intelligence, talents, sensitivity and pursuit of peace and serenity.

Her writing talents in her senior year of college won her the runner-up position in the *Mademoiselle* magazine Prix de Paris contest. Much as she would have loved first place and actual time in Paris, Claudia was thrilled with her prize. She got to work for *Vogue* and *Mademoiselle* magazines in New York for six months. Claudia loved these fashion magazines and the fashion industry. She was well suited to the artistic fast track in New York where she shared a little loft apartment in Greenwich Village.

Collect calls to Mother started coming on a regular basis, for a mattress, for winter clothes. Mother's quietly squirreled-away resources were quickly depleted. Eventually she had to set Claudia's plights and pleas in front of Dad. Dad, tired by the collect calls and the next dollar amount requested, took the phone from Mom and told Claudia that he had educated his daughters so that they'd be better able to provide for themselves. If she couldn't take care of herself in New York, she should come home. He had two more kids to educate. He wasn't sending any more money. He forbade mother to send any more money. If Claudia couldn't work it out, he'd send her a plane ticket home.

Mother, on the other hand, having heard Claudia weep through so many protestations of, "What's the point of living if I can't follow my dreams?" was as compliant as she could be to Claudia's requests and pleadings. Mother clearly didn't discount these pleadings as potential threats of suicide. Claudia's financial requests were attached to prompting Mother to demonstrate love. Claudia didn't resist saying, "If you don't send the money, you don't love me," or "If you love me, send the money." That usually worked. Claudia epitomized far better than most of us, "when there's a will, there's a way."

Winning the contest, working at the magazines, meeting famous people, making connections and living in Greenwich Village was a dream that Claudia made a reality. When the prize period was over she somehow managed to get back to Florida. There, in addition to continuing to paint, she became an assistant-instructor in deep sea diving. A couple of her salt-water swimming stories included having fishes nibble at her gold earrings and being stung by a Man-o-War. Such episodes may have contributed to her career change.

Searches/Seductions/Losses

G etting to Paris became Claudia's next goal. A friend who was applying for a stewardess position encouraged Claudia to apply too. Pan American Airlines hired her. Most of her flight assignments were to Mexico, a country with history, artists, artworks and culture that she loved. But she did also get to France with museums, menus, wines and romance that she loved even more. A prince and a shah were among the airlines passengers she met. It made her sad to learn from them and from others of significant means that wealth didn't make them happy.

Although she was able to travel, she didn't like the job. She didn't like the uniforms. She didn't like the sad rich people who didn't find interests in life that would make them appreciate their money. The stewardess job robbed her of time she could be painting. She needed to focus on her artwork and make it work for her.

That produced another period of her collect calls to Mother. Claudia also disclosed to Mother various unedited stories about her friends. She always boasted of being totally open and honest about her opinions and her interactions with people. Claudia's favorite friend at the time was a man who she described as sweet and worldly-wise. He lived on his sailboat. He offered himself to be her mentor, and she was learning much of value from him. He was about the same age as Daddy.

The news of an older man in Claudia's life further disinclined our own daddy from sending any of his or Mother's hard-earned income to his errant daughter. Dad, who was not a person of practiced correspondence, sent Claudia several letters basically stating that she had gone awry in life and better come home to get straightened out. Claudia somehow managed to keep partying and paying the rent in Florida.

I was seventeen when Claudia flew home for a few days. She came with Doug, not an old man but a man who'd proposed marriage to her. He was a military man in charge of a guided-missile base in the Bahamas. They flew home in his personal Piper-Cub. Doug wanted to meet our family; and then they'd fly to California to meet his family. He saw these as sensible things to do before they got married.

Doug was handsome, confident and amiable with all of us. He scored high marks with me when he said in front of my parents that he thought I was more mature and realistic than Claudia. But he said Claudia had won his heart and was the intriguing personality he wanted to marry.

Claudia for those three days was testy, easily annoyed, and as I recall didn't smile or demonstrate good humor even once. She wasn't at all happy with me. By that time, what had been my big sisters' room was my bedroom. Claudia was clearly annoyed to have to share it with me. She was even more annoyed when I asked to borrow a fashion T-shirt from her suitcase. She resisted. I persisted. Finally, with clear instructions on how she expected it back with no snags, stains or damage, she let me borrow it. Unfortunately at the party someone's cherry coke did get splashed on me. When I arrived home, Claudia noticed the stain which repeated washing did not remove. Claudia let me keep the damaged goods, with the admonition that I was never to borrow anything of hers ever again.

A few days after Claudia and Doug flew on to California, Mother got a phone call. She reported to us that Claudia and Doug had gotten married in California and would be visiting us again on their return trip to Florida. For the day or two she and Doug were with us Claudia pretty much sequestered herself in our bedroom, sharing it with me rather than Doug. She sobbed nearly the whole time, and blew her nose noisily day and night. She told me she didn't want to talk about anything. She told me that Doug had forced himself on her and forced her to marry him, and that she had never been so miserable.

When they got back to Florida, Doug called to report that he had checked Claudia into a hospital. She had hepatitis that had turned to jaundice. She was a very sick girl. Her illness was clearly the cause of all her sobbing unhappy behavior. They expected the hospitalization to last at least six weeks.

Before Claudia checked out of the hospital, Doug found her a cheery, charming little apartment and bought her a '54 red MGB so that she'd have an easy means of transportation as she regained her strength. Claudia was pleased indeed with both the apartment and the car. Perhaps she had married the right man after all.

It wasn't long, however, before Doug became tired of flights back from his military assignment in the Bahamas to Florida for weekends with Claudia. She was aghast at his suggestion that they build a cottage on the Bahama beach which would not have access to electricity or running water. When Claudia made clear that such a plan was totally unacceptable, Doug started looking for alternatives that might be affordable in the Bahamas. They became aware that connections with a real estate attorney and some political connection in the Bahamas would be necessary.

Claudia called Mother with an unexpected invitation to come visit. Surprisingly Mother booked a flight and flew to Florida. While there, Claudia further suggested that they fly to Nassau together so that Claudia could find out who to contact and how to attain title to land there. They'd been in Nassau a couple days when Claudia told Mother that she'd run into friends who invited her to sail with them back to Miami. Mother flew home without obtaining any particulars such as the name of the people Claudia was sailing with or the identity of the boat.

When the call came a couple days later from Doug asking, "Where's Claudia?" Mother was stunned. Doug had come home for the weekend on his customary schedule and found no wife, no note, and no message. He became furious that Mother could provide him no names, no boat identity, and no designated sailing route. As soon as that call ended, Mother called the Florida Coast Guard to report her daughter missing at sea. She couldn't provide them helpful information to commence their search. The only solace she gained was their immediate information that they had retrieved no body fitting Claudia's description in the number of days that had passed since the time Mother left Nassau. Mother was beside herself. This potential horror held sway over our household for a couple more days. We all tried to quell our imaginations as we reflected back on hearing Mother say, "My daughter is missing at sea."

The relief was enormous when Claudia called to say that she was fine. Her continuing report that they'd had fun and a great sail back and that no one needed to have worried was not well received by anyone. Mother was highly agitated by such flippancy and lack of understanding of the duress she'd caused. Dad was disgusted and intentionally demeaning to his daughter. And Doug was enraged. Our family learned shortly thereafter that for Doug this caper was the last straw. He could never forgive her. He no longer wanted her as his wife. The marriage had lasted nine months.

Claudia gave up the darling apartment, stored her paintings and art supplies with various friends, packed up her clothes, and spent three days driving the wonderful red MG home through nearly non-stop rainstorms. She, the car, and all her clothes arrived at home soaked. She was happy to be done with Doug, but clearly she wasn't happy to be home. That was simply a necessity until decisions were made about what and where she would go and do next. I wasn't privy to the conversations and decisions, but in less than a month she was driving back to Florida. Focus on my own college education experiences and romances took precedence, and I had little awareness of what went on in Claudia's life for the next four or five years.

*   *   *   *   *

For nine years after her soaked MG visit home, I didn't see her. Sometime in that interim Claudia met and married Max, an oceanographer. To our knowledge there wasn't any wedding ceremony, just the processing of legal documents constituting a marriage. Her husband was Jewish so she converted to Reform Judaism even though he didn't practice his religion. His parents were Orthodox Jews who never accepted her.

On a business trip to Florida, Brett went to visit Claudia and Max. He reported that Claudia was a totally changed person. She no longer smoked or drank. She was into natural juices and health foods. She was greatly subdued in her behavior and seemed serious but happy. Brett said next to nothing about Claudia's husband except that he seemed like a nice guy. Brett was primarily puzzled and intrigued about the transformation of his big sister.

Claudia's marriage to the oceanographer lasted five years. Brett was the only member of our family who ever met Max face to face. I never even saw a photograph of him. It was strange to think that I might inadvertently encounter some fellow somewhere and never know that this person was once my brother-in-law.

Decades later Claudia filled in much missing information about her second marriage. It was actually the MG from Doug that led to her meeting Max who also had an MG. In those days people who had the same brand or model of sports car automatically waved and/or tooted at each other. Claudia was teaching art at various elementary schools, driving daily to one or another. She and Max would regularly pass, toot and wave at each other on the road. Claudia also regularly stopped at a small roadside restaurant to have a cup of coffee and a croissant on her way to work.

As Claudia told me this story she was well on her way to getting sloshed. Her semi-drunken condition seemed to add to her enjoyment of reflecting on these earlier days of drinking. She said that at that time her group of friends partied every night at the Club. She laughed about having such terrible hangovers every morning that she wore her sunglasses while she taught. She talked about wearing her sunglasses at the morning coffee bar too.

One morning there were no available seating spaces along the coffee bar. As she looked around the room she saw a fellow she recognized from the nightly drinking group she was a part of. He was seated with another man, and he beckoned her to join them. The other man was Max. He in turn recognized her as the girl with the MG. In addition to being an oceanographer he owned a cocktail bar. Though Max did little drinking, his social skills suited bar ownership.

Claudia at that time was sharing what she called a "shack" with a girlfriend. Max was living in a shabby garage apartment. Their romance advanced and several factors prompted her to suggest to Max that he marry her. She was haunted by the perpetual prospect that she'd become pregnant. She thought monogamy and marriage went together. They enjoyed cooking and so many other things together that she thought they should combine households and live together. Since his father insisted that he have a Jewish wife, and since Claudia felt her own religious background of what she called an atheist father and a fervently religious mother was unhealthy for children, Claudia would convert to Judaism. Claudia hated Max's shabby apartment as well as her shack, so she found a house for them to buy. She needed to borrow an unstated amount from Mother for that and never mentioned if any repayment terms and conditions were attached to it.

Relatively early in the marriage Max had a business conference in Chicago. He said he would combine it with a little side trip to meet Claudia's parents. Claudia's report of that wasn't clear as to whether Max simply phoned her folks or met with them. Basically whatever happened Dad told Claudia, "You will never be as intelligent as he is."

The subject of intelligence both ranked high and rankled our family. In our family headed by schoolteacher parents, IQ came through as a valid measuring tool. All of us were aware that Claudia had the highest IQ of the four children. It didn't rank her with Einstein, but it did entitle her to an elite status. For Dad to rank Max higher than Claudia on the intelligence scale was something Claudia found unforgivable.

In her marriage to Max, Claudia observed that the marriage itself was a turning point in Max's attitude. They didn't cook and do grocery shopping together anymore. He saw those as her exclusive wifely duties. Laughter and fun subsided pretty quickly, and no potential pregnancy materialized. In this dissipation of happiness, Claudia became physically ill. A friend advised her to take a leave of absence from her teaching job. He also told her of a psychiatrist he thought might help her with the perplexities she was feeling. The counseling would basically be free as part of her medical leave-of-absence.

At her first meeting with the psychiatrist Claudia stated that she doubted he could be of any value to her. She told him she was unhappy, but there was nothing to resolve it. He asked her what made her unhappy, and she simply burst into tears. Then she sobbed and blew her nose depleting two entire boxes of Kleenex. Claudia added no details. The emphasis was on "two entire boxes of Kleenex."

She continued to see the psychiatrist once a week. Eventually she disclosed to him that much of her unhappiness was about Max and his lack of interests. An example was travel. Claudia loved to travel and wanted to take a trip each year. Max wasn't interested, didn't view that as his husbandly duty, and said she could take the annual trips by herself. The first year she did that and joined a travel group to Mexico City that went on to San Miguel de Allende. She loved it. She socialized, danced, sang, and felt alive. She didn't want to go back home to Max where she felt no life. But she did return home.

Her psychiatrist said perhaps he should see Max. He did for one session. Max confirmed that Claudia's observations of him and his lack of compatible interests was correct. There appeared to be no solutions to her happiness issues in that department.

Claudia told her psychiatrist that she'd always been confused about sex. She knew that most people were enthused about it and ranked it as an important activity, but she'd never found it pleasurable. The doctor noted that she'd had quite a number of sexual experiences. Claudia attributed that to her seeking to understand and find a satisfying solution to this aspect of life.

Claudia told me that she fell in love with her psychiatrist and tried to seduce him, which he declined in deference to his wife. In any case, after months of seeing the psychiatrist Claudia was finding no solutions to her unhappiness. She went to her session planning to inform the doctor that she was done and wouldn't be back. Before her planned exit, he asked what made her happy. Claudia said, "Then the most amazing thing happened. I looked at him and he turned into a golden Buddha, all shimmering. I looked at it for a while and then it disappeared and he was sitting there."

"How did you do that?" she said.

He asked, "How did I do what?"

When Claudia told him that he had just been a beautiful shimmering golden Buddha like one she used to touch in Chicago's Art Institute, he asked her more about it. She explained that in high school and ever since, the Asian exhibits and the Buddhas were her favorites. As a teenager she knew she wasn't supposed to touch them, but she did when no one else was around. She had a magical sense when she even thought about that introduction to Buddhism and Asian art in the Art Institute. The doctor encouraged her to read and study Eastern religions. She saw him for a total of about nine months. Then he moved to New York. Claudia said she gave him the best small painting she thought she'd ever done and never had further contact with him. She never again went to a therapist.

*   *   *   *   *

About the time of Claudia's divorce from Max, Brett took a job in southern California. Claudia packed up her personal possessions and decided to head to the West Coast too. She landed a job teaching art in West Hollywood. She stayed with Brett until he told her to find her own place. Brett said she was back to her old self and loved to go drinking and dancing with him, but she was a crimp on his bachelor life.

Claudia rented a tiny guest house located next to the wonderful swimming pool on the grounds of an estate. Mother shared the photographs of Claudia's new home. It looked like a delightful dollhouse decorated with Claudia's charming artistic touches.

Other than Christmas and birthday cards, and receiving mini-reports about Claudia from other family members, I was out of touch with Claudia. During that long period Claudia found that she far preferred California to Florida. She taught elementary school art year after year, kept up her own painting and photography, and took exotic-destination trips every summer or vacation period. To learn more of Zen Buddhism, she traveled to Japan. To learn more of Hinduism, she traveled throughout India. Then she explored the histories, cultures and religious practices in Bali, Sri Lanka, Thailand and Cambodia. Angkor Wat was breathtaking artistically and spiritually, a fabulous dream come true for Claudia.

She also traveled to Russia while it was still Soviet to experience a country under communism and its suppression of the Russian Orthodox religion. She traveled to Stonehenge and to other mystical sites. Egypt and Kenya fulfilled other elements of her travel agenda. She landed and completed a commission to do interior murals in the dining rooms of the Kenya Safari Club.

When she was teaching in California and exploring the world's cultures and religions in the summers, remarkably she saved enough money to buy her first charming little house. She said she bought it outright with her savings, but there were later disclosures of a substantial contribution from Mother. It was a pretty white house with green trim in Pacific Palisades with a small yard for flower gardens. Claudia was steadily pursuing her dreams.

Claudia declined to come to my wedding. She said that she didn't go any more to weddings or funerals. She said that when she attended events she liked to be the center of attention and that she'd learned that didn't work well at weddings and funerals. She did however send a large wedding painting she'd done of me, and later she gave us several of her paintings of Mexican scenes.

We established a semi-regular correspondence. My newsy letters were so unlike her philosophical and advisory ones. She wrote them on art paper on which she'd water-colored a delightful self-portrait in various costumes and characters, signed "Claudette." I encouraged her to put her Claudette cards into production to create an additional line of income to offset her perpetual complaint of insufficient funds. She declined, saying it would rob her of time for her big paintings. Her paintings, not cards, were the road to fame and fortune that she was so dedicated to achieving.

I had my collection of "Claudettes" matted and framed. When she arrived to leave Jouster with us, she was pleased to see them and the prominent places her other artworks occupied in our house. But then she reprimanded me for disclosing to her the faces, figures and hidden elements I saw in her paintings. She told me that artists hated to hear inane observations like mine. Her comment dropped on me like the guillotine, a beheaded footnote.

*   *   *   *   *

Life went on, and new life came. Four years after Tom and I were married our first child, Zachary arrived. I sustained a neck injury similar to whiplash during childbirth, but was delighted that the baby was strong and healthy. A devastating misfortune was that the first death in our immediate family happened at the same time.

Since there was a phone in my hospital room, I found it strange that Tom was called out of the room to take what the nurse said was an emergency call. I simply knew that whatever it was would be very bad news. My speculation was that my father had died. Dad had had his first heart attack just before Thanksgiving during my sophomore year at UW. I didn't learn about it until I arrived home for the holiday. Dad was on a bed that had been moved downstairs. Surprisingly, Dad immediately followed the doctor's orders to give up smoking. He even more surprisingly gave up drinking all forms of alcohol after his second heart attack a few years later. In my hospital room with my new baby I felt certain that my father's death was the news poor Tom would have to deliver to me when he came back in the room. As Tom entered I said, "It's my dad, isn't it."

"No," he said with a pause, "your brother."

Stunned and not knowing the real meaning, I went on, "Where is he? Is he badly hurt? Was it a car accident? Will he be alright?"

And Tom simply said, "He's dead."

Then he told me it was Elli's husband who called, because Brett had been living in Cleveland where their family lived. Brett had been playing squash with a friend at the Cleveland Athletic Club. They sat on a bench after several games, taking a breather before they resumed. Standing up to resume playing, Brett said to his friend, "Boy, you sure know how to wear a guy out," and he simply collapsed to the floor.

A trainer was called in immediately to commence CPR, and several doctors at the club came to help, but Brett was gone. They called it "athlete's heart," the kind of thing you hear of usually in high school athletics in football or basketball games. It's sudden and final. My brother was dead. There was nothing even the most knowledgeable doctor could have done to restore his life. Elli and her family had arranged a memorial service in Cleveland because Brett had made so many friends there. Basically they needed the memorial service to help their four kids through the tragedy of losing their favorite Uncle Brett who spent so much time with them.

Stunned by the news, and restrained by my malfunctioning neck, I couldn't move or get a grip on my whirling thoughts and emotions. I must have said, "Do my folks and Claudia know?"

Tom answered, "Elli and Doug called your folks. Your mom let Claudia know. That's all I know."

I asked, "How can we get to the memorial service?"

Tom responded, "We'll probably learn more tomorrow. You can ask your doctor then. Take good care of yourself and the little guy tonight. I can't be here until after work tomorrow."

When the doctor made his rounds entering my room the next afternoon asking, "How are you doing," I burst into uncontrollable tears and sobbing. Eventually I got enough words out to tell him of my brother's death and of the memorial service planned in Cleveland.

The doctor, shocked by the news and by the emotional demeanor he'd never before experienced from me, responded, "I can't release you from the hospital until you can naturally lift your head, and until your milk has come in and nursing is steady. I'm sorry, but with your injury and a new baby, it's not advisable for you to travel."

It was three days before I was released from the hospital. By then Tom's mother had arrived to stay with us for my first week at home with Zachary. She prepared all the meals and managed the general household.

She also brought the gift of Rachel Carson's <u>Book of Wonder</u>. She gave it to me after lunch. As I opened it and started to read I was overwhelmed with emotion. Tears rolled down my cheeks and I couldn't suppress sobbing. That reaction was another cycle of the devastation I felt from Brett's death. Unable to speak of that, as I fled from the room I heard her explain to Tom, "I'm so sorry. Its post-partum depression, but common and should pass away in a few days."

I felt particularly alone having lost my brother. It was time for me to reconnect and strengthen my connections with my sisters. When I called Elli there was an immediate sense of connection between us. We began the healing process of sharing our grief.

Greatly heartened by the sympathy, comfort and sense of sisterliness in my call with Elli, I called Claudia. I started by saying, "I'm finally home from the hospital, so this is the first chance I've had to call."

"That's good," she said, "I'm glad that you and the baby are fine."

"Well I can't say I'm fine, I answered. "My neck is still healing as are my stitches. Tom's mom is here to help, but she gave me Rachel Carson's <u>Book of Wonder</u>, and when I started to read it, all I could do was to think of Brett. I just fell apart and couldn't stop crying. Tom's mom doesn't seem to understand that I've lost my brother. That's why I was crying. The book overwhelmed me with memories. She thinks I have post-partum depression."

Claudia cut in, "I knew there had been a terrible tragedy even before I got the call about Brett. I was doing a reading with my Tarot cards. I drew the Death Card. I thought it meant that you had died in childbirth. I knew the date was your due date."

My mind flashed on imaginings of people who go to psychics, sit around tables with crystal balls, and play with Ouiji Boards. Why was Claudia doing a Tarot reading on my due date?

She continued, "You know Brettie was always my favorite in our family. I had so many happy experiences with him. We shared a lot of good times."

I responded, "I didn't know you took the Tarot cards so seriously."

"Oh, yes," she said, "I've had my astrological chart done too, but it takes a very knowledgeable person to do an astrological chart correctly. You should have yours done."

I replied, "Mother can't recall what time of day I was born, and it's not listed on my birth certificate, so I can't have a chart done."

Claudia was silent, so I went on, "Because Tom was called out, rather than using the phone in my room, I sensed that something was amiss, that the call had to be very bad news. I thought Dad had died. I just couldn't believe it was Brett. I felt so bad for Mother and Dad. Mother told me that Dad was pleased that I used our family name as Zachary's middle name. Brett was the end of the line for our family name."

With Claudia again silent in my pause, I was glad when she finally said, "Well I'm glad that you and the baby are fine."

Having come full-circle in our conversation, I took the cue to sign off. "I'm glad you're okay too," I said. "Stay in touch."

For me an immediate connection with my sister Claudia didn't occur, nor did the sharing of grief, as it had with Elli. I thought it was outrageous of Claudia to put such merit in the Tarot cards. I felt angry that she was checking the cards on my due date to see if I had died in childbirth. And, yes, I thought Claudia's message was that the wrong sibling had died.

Six months later on Brett's birthday, our Dad died. Claudia didn't come for his memorial service either. Six months after that, our paternal grandmother died. Three deaths from three generations was a rough road for me in that year and a half. Perhaps Claudia experienced it as spiritual growth. She said she'd discontinued Tarot Cards when Brett died.

*   *   *   *   *

The following year Claudia agreed to come join us for the Christmas holidays, forewarned that Mother would be with us. This time, she left the dog with a friend. She brought year-old Zachary a wonderful Steiff stuffed toy. That may have been the first year she also brought a Babar the Elephant book, the start of a collection to which she added for several years.

Among other things Tom and I had planned a ski outing with her while Mother would baby-sit with Zachary. Claudia came to breakfast with a sour face. Even though the ski outing had been her request in our pre-Christmas phone calls, she, at that last moment made it clear that she didn't want to go skiing. Tom piped in that we were going. When I went to my room to get into ski clothes, she came in. I was cornered as she spat out, "You're not going to leave me here alone all day with Mother!" If I went skiing, she would never forgive me; if I stayed home, my husband would be furious. He'd taken a rare day off from work, because Claudia had told us of how much she loved to ski. Tom detested Claudia's power plays and my giving in to them.

With much agony I told Claudia I was going skiing. Claudia closed herself in her room. Mom told us to have fun. Tom and I left for what proved to be a distracted, non-pleasurable day for me. When we arrived home, Mother was her sweet self. Claudia was quiet. Before bedtime Claudia told me that she had written two poems that she'd left on my pillow. After everyone had settled down for the night, I read them. They were very sad and beautiful poems that made tears roll silently down my cheeks.

At breakfast the next day I thanked her for the poems and told her they were beautiful. To myself I marveled at her ability to pull such a rabbit out of the hat after the turmoil that provoked them. But I was at a complete loss to understand what really had caused such a ruckus, and I knew she had no idea of how demanding and demeaning she had been.

There was another Christmas or two that Claudia visited us while Zachary and his brother Clarke were tots. When the boys were ages five and three, Claudia told me that I lacked good techniques in mothering and was totally failing to teach my boys manners. She further said the damage I was doing to my sons would cause Zachary in particular to be in therapy for the rest of his life. I found these judgments devastating. No matter how much logic and reason were missing from her statements, the wound had been delivered. It took me decades to realize that the favoritism she had for Clarke and the aspersions she cast on Zak were in direct context with her childhood relationship with Elli.

On one of those Christmas trips Claudia arrived in a full-length dark brown ermine coat. I didn't stifle my curiosity about how she'd afforded such an extravagance. Eventually she disclosed that it was a gift from her male friend. This was the first I had heard about him, so I pressed her to tell me more. He often played tennis with her at the country club. Though they went to many music concerts and events as well as their tennis games, Claudia was adamant that there was no romance or sexual element to their relationship. He was a married man whose wife had been confined in mental institutions for years with no hope for recovery.

Claudia was annoyed at all my questions. When I asked about her annoyance, she said that she was considering that her relationship with the fellow ought to be over. They had a major argument, content undisclosed, about a week before she came for Christmas. She didn't know if or when they might be back on speaking terms.

When I called Claudia a couple weeks after she returned to California she had just learned that her male friend had died suddenly. Claudia was furious with the circle of friends who knew, but hadn't the courtesy to let her know of his death. If Claudia had remorse about her argument with him, or sorrow about his death, she didn't say so. Her focus was on justifying her anger that others had waited so long to tell her he died.

Birthday cards, Christmas cards, infrequent letters and phone calls occupied more than the next decade of my relationship with Claudia. No more visits.

Intoxication/Tirades/Tap Tests

My dive into a serious depression related to the circumstances that brought my seventeen-year marriage to Tom to an end, prompted Claudia to re-enter my life. When she learned about my level of suffering she stepped in as my self-appointed champion. I received long letters almost daily, frequently four pages both sides. Various words, phrases or whole sentences would be underlined and loaded with multiple exclamation points. The letters waxed poetic philosophically between tirades against Tom and strongly parental-type guidance about what to think or do, or what not to think or do. Many people including professional therapists were helping to save my life at that time. I have to count Claudia strongly among them. Elli, via trading phone calls every few days, was a soothing and steadying support too.

Shortly after my divorce, a Milwaukee friend invited me to be her guest along with her two kids at the Sands in Las Vegas. I'd never been to Vegas, was touched by the generous invitation, and composed my air itinerary to include a few days visit with Claudia in her new house in Carmel.

We had three gleeful days. I had never been anywhere in California and Carmel was a heady introduction. Claudia's little wooden cottage house was in the wooded hills, walking distance from town center. Her house was charming, full of her artworks, a gallery of them, as well as her vast collection of art books. The living room featured a large, cream-colored, macramé hammock, Claudia's favorite spot to relax and read. Her bedroom was large, very feminine, with a king-sized bed with a French floral bedspread and lacy decorative pillows. Her jade pendants and other jewelry pieces hung on the wall next to her hand-painted bureau and mirror. By the front door of the house was a Rosemaled plaque of hearts and flowers with the words Casa Claudia. The garage was simply storage space, a substitute for the attics and basements we have in the Midwest.

The guest bedroom where I stayed had a twin-sized trundle bed and a massive collection of little pillows, stuffed animals and dolls. It was a small, perfect room for a four or eight year-old girl. At the time I visited Claudia she was forty-eight and I was thirty-nine. Having a room of childhood reverie was perfect for me as a "recovering adult." It also rekindled my only comfort and caring memory of Claudia in my early childhood, the one time when I was two or three recovering from the flu. Instead of her customary rejection of me, she had carried me downstairs, sat down with me in her lap as she read a portion of an Oz book to me. On this exceptional occasion she was being nice to her little sister.

Claudia's house had a picket fence and an additional fence between the corner of the house and the garage that separated off the side garden. The side garden had a small brick courtyard surrounded by thriving rose plants and agapanthus. It also had a chaise lounge for sunbathing, and a couple wrought iron ice-cream parlor chairs. The house behind and the next-door house both were at much higher elevations and were separated from Claudia's property by concrete walls. Claudia's courtyard side garden was quite private. It was also the containment area for replacement-Jouster who could go in and out at will from the little dog door in her living room.

Claudia played classical music tapes from the time she awoke until bedtime. She served hot tea, fresh berries and miniature croissants for breakfast. I picked up the tab for our various meals and excursions. Casanova's Restaurant in Carmel still ranks at the top of my favorite restaurants. Clint Eastwood's Hog's Breath restaurant-bar and The Lodge in Pebble Beach were among our excursions. Her best friend at the time was Victoria whose mother still had the family home with remarkable ocean views in Pebble Beach. Claudia and I, sometimes with Victoria, strolled through all the art galleries in Carmel and attended wine and cheese receptions at several of them. We drank white wine from noon onward, at home, at meals, at gallery openings, anywhere for any reason. Claudia regularly set the scene for fascinating conversations or dialogs which turned into the monologues she then delivered.

Nonetheless the three days were fabulous, full of activity, animations, smiles and laughter, great food, fine wine and for me, a whole new world and the best time I'd ever had with Claudia.

A few months later Elli called to say that she was going to a conference in San Francisco and thought she would combine it with a visit at Claudia's. Not comfortable with being alone with Claudia, she asked if I could manage to go too. This was an opportunity I couldn't pass up. It would be the first time the three of us had been together in thirty years! Thirty years earlier was when Claudia had been Maid-of-Honor and I a flower girl in Elli's wedding. After twenty-seven years of marriage Elli and Ross had been divorced. All of us at this point in our lives like it or not, had been divorced, Claudia twice. This gathering was an enticement for rebuilding family.

I arrived at Claudia's the day before Elli did. Not knowing weather for northern California in April, I brought my most summery clothes. They were totally inappropriate for the cold, damp, non-Californian weather I encountered. Claudia found some wool slacks in her closet that fit me and loaned me a couple sweaters, jackets, even warm pajamas during the week we were scheduled to stay. And this time Claudia announced that I would share her bed and let Elli have the guestroom. Claudia felt that her childhood and sharing a bedroom with Elli had been a sufficient penance.

Smoking was a habit of mine that Claudia hated. My smoking, as I had voluntarily done during my prior visit, was relegated to outdoors. This time I even brought my own small-lidded ashtray that I could carry to dispose of butts at curbside trash containers. Nonetheless Claudia was relentless in her criticism of my smoking despite my keeping it to a minimum.

Though Claudia had driven her car to pick me up at the airport, I was surprised she wasn't doing the same for Elli. Elli took a cab. For the life of me, I can't recall what exactly transpired in the first half-hour or so that the three of us were together. It only took that long for my childhood memories of my sisters' relationship to be recreated. They were in a major harangue with Elli asserting that she'd call a cab and take the next plane out. I pleaded with them both not to let this happen. I assured them that whatever had transpired in our childhood didn't have to prevail over this new circumstance. I asserted that we were all grownups now and that squabbling was unbecoming to women of our ages.

In retrospect that initial band aid I put on the situation was pathetically naïve. The entire week was a wild emotional roller-coaster ride for all of us. Despite some hours of calm and even some of laughter and fun, the spontaneous and unbecoming squabbling between Claudia and Elli repeatedly accelerated into shouting and tears. Fortunately the shouting matches and rages for the most part stayed in Claudia's house and out of public view. Our excursions into town and the area weren't exempt, however, from seething sessions. Fortunately whoever was ready to explode took a break to the nearest powder room, or a walk around the block.

I needed my walk around the block one night when we went out to dinner. Claudia ordered an after-dinner drink for herself; and I decided, with others smoking nearby us, to have a cigarette at the table. I'd just lit it when Claudia grabbed it, tore it in pieces and threw it in the ashtray. I equally outrageously lit up another. Claudia did the same thing to it, except this time she threw it on the floor. I took an immediate exit for my walk around the block. I could hear Elli reprimanding Claudia for causing a scene.

Claudia's behavior was particularly astounding since she had forewarned us that Carmel was actually a gossipy small town in atmosphere. She said that people noticed what other people wore and how they behaved, and she certainly hoped that neither of us would embarrass her. After all, we were going back home, but she lived there and would have to live with the embarrassment. For her to be tearing up and throwing around my cigarette in a place where a lot of people were smoking, I thought would qualify as embarrassing herself. But, Claudia drank a lot of wine that may have moderated her interpretations of embarrassment.

Elli and I were embarrassed at Claudia's behavior another night. We'd stopped for nightcaps. Claudia started a conversation at the bar with a fellow who evidently conveyed to her that he had some back pain. Since Claudia believed herself to be a healer of such things she commenced giving this fellow a back massage. This was no quick fix. Claudia massaged more and more extensively picking up on none of our hints to disengage from this activity. Instead she apologized to the fellow about our interference. We wondered what gossip might flow about this episode.

Our three-sister conversations at other times were revealing. When Claudia told Elli how horrendous it has been for her to wait for Elli to finish college before she herself could go to school, Elli topped that. She told Claudia of how horrendous it was for Elli, the first-born favorite, to be told by Daddy Bunch, our grandfather, that when Claudia came along she became his favorite. Though many such thoughtless things are conveyed to children, childhood memories of such messages are dangerous and damaging.

Claudia obviously contemplated Elli's story overnight. At breakfast the next day Claudia apologized to Elli for Grampa's behavior. Claudia went on to say that she always knew she was Daddy Bunches favorite, but she hadn't known how cruel he had been toward little Elli in telling her so. Claudia said further that the story explained why Elli had always hated her.

From my perspective, though Elli seemed pleased by Claudia's apology, there was also a lot of self-aggrandizement in the telling. It was a double-edged sword. Elli was entitled to experience the hurt from what Daddy Bunch had said, but Daddy Bunch had told the truth. Claudia was his favorite. Somehow Elli got caught up in the moment of sympathy and not in the message, "but the truth is that Claudia is cuter, quicker and more interesting than you are."

Perhaps Elli later realized and felt the other edge of the sword. Elli asserted to Claudia that Claudia was an alcoholic. Elli knew a lot about it because Ross was an alcoholic and Elli had gone through all of the Al-Anon training and support activities.

Claudia was furious at Elli's assertion. Claudia talked about life being such a difficult struggle, about people being so stupid and uncaring, about a glass of wine or two softening the edges of all these misfortunes.

Elli didn't relent. She stated that Claudia was a wino, an escapist through drink, a maintainer of her own facades, a person who built a wall between herself and any meaningful relationships. Claudia, who by then was at a stage of slurred speech, said that she was always able to safely drive home, and that she might drink a bit too much on occasion, but was not an alcoholic, simply a Californian.

Claudia went on in a sadly serious manner to say that she always knew that one day the two of us, her two sisters, would show up on her doorstep and need her to take care of us. Claudia was masterful at these sudden changes of direction.

After Claudia dropped us off at the airport the next day, Elli and I wondered how Claudia could perceive that we'd shown up on her doorstep and what she thought she'd done to take care of us. My hopes of forging a triumvirate, a supportive sisterhood of reason and mutual respect were proven ridiculous. It was outrageous that any three adult women could have produced the volatile week the three of us had just experienced. The concept of any future three-way reunion for any reason was out of the question.

We had, however, one area of agreement. Our mother after eight years of widowhood had an old beau, Clarence, show up to court her. At age seventy-two she married him. Elli and I were her bridesmaids; my boys served as ring bearers. Other than the couple of Christmases when Claudia came to my house in Milwaukee, mother hadn't seen Claudia. Claudia followed her "weddings and funerals" policy and didn't attend Mother's wedding. A couple years later Clarence and Mother visited Claudia in Carmel. Claudia found Clarence boring and judgmental. Furthermore Clarence was childless in his prior fifty-year marriage, was very possessive of Mother and treated her attention to her adult daughters as unreasonable competition. Negative observations about Clarence were something we three sisters held in common.

*   *   *   *   *

Elli visited Claudia one more time about five years later. By then Elli was engaged to Sven. I was surprised to learn from Elli that Claudia declined to have them stay together in her house because they were an unmarried couple. That was typical of the dichotomies Claudia represented. Her own behavior vacillated between promiscuous and prudish, just as her ideas ranged from profound to picayune. Claudia picked and chose at her own convenience when to timidly worry about what the neighbors thought or to audaciously flaunt, "Why give a damn about them!"

Elli and Sven's visit to Carmel was only for three days, mostly in activities independent of Claudia. Elli reported, "Claudia is drinking like a fish." Otherwise, Elli thought the visit went smoothly.

Claudia reported that it went smoothly too. Claudia also reiterated her anger thesis, as she had when Elli got cancer and had reconstructive surgery after her mastectomy. She said that Elli was basically an angry person, and that's what caused her cancer. Other than Claudia's soothsaying, Elli, the smiling, cheerful, fun-loving person, would not be commonly described as harboring anger.

Elli had vented and put to rest negative childhood memories and jealousies about Claudia, but she hadn't overcome anger about a more recent incident with Claudia. Our elderly Uncle George and Aunt Priscilla had called Elli and asked her to consider moving in with them in their home in Naples, Florida. They wanted her to provide them assistance and companionship for their remaining years. Priscilla and George never had kids of their own. They'd give Elli their Cadillac in which they'd need occasional chauffeuring to medical appointments, and they'd make her sole inheritor of their estate worth about half a million at that time. Elli told them it was a generous and tempting offer that she would think through.

Elli lived near two of her four kids and now also had little grandchildren she adored. She needed to weigh that and also to have her fiancé, Sven, weigh-in on the proposal. She knew Sven loved her and was committed to being a monogamous couple. Though Sven was willing for them to be permanently engaged, Elli thought he would probably always avoid the official status of marriage. If he was willing to go with her to fulfill George and Priscilla's proposal, then she'd see if that was also suitable with them. If Sven wasn't willing to go, then she would re-evaluate the Florida proposal as something for her to decide independently. Entering this new life in Florida could be a workable option. She and Sven decided that he could set up a chiropractic office in Naples. They could be a team in helping George and Priscilla. They'd sort through the pros and cons during the next couple weeks and probably accept. At that time Elli was convinced of her clean bill of health after her bout with breast cancer.

When Claudia heard about this offer she called George and Priscilla. She told Priscilla that she'd always felt an affinity with her because Priscilla was an art lover, a watercolor portraitist, and a collector of lovely things from the Orient. Claudia told them that she couldn't leave her job or abandon the time she spent on artworks. She said she'd love to have them move to Carmel. They could choose from several lovely condo developments there within easy driving distance for Claudia to visit them a couple times a week.

They told Claudia that their offer to Elli was contingent upon their staying in their home to maintain being in touch with a long-established group of friends and neighbors who'd visit them. They weren't interested in moving to California.

When they said they were awaiting Elli's decision, Claudia told them that Elli hadn't told them the whole story. Claudia said that between Elli's cancer, and the fact that Elli was engaged, it was unlikely that Elli was seriously thinking of moving in with them as their caretaker.

George and Priscilla were stunned and angered by Claudia's disclosures. It made them feel that Elli hadn't been forthright with them and made them hold onto false hopes. In Elli's next call to me she read me the scathing letter she'd just received from George and Priscilla. It referenced their call from Claudia in which they'd learned how deceiving Elli had been with them. That Elli hadn't mentioned her cancer or the status of her love life was commensurate to lying. She had caused them to hold onto false hopes that were now dashed. They had no interest in hearing anything further from her.

Elli was deeply hurt by the insinuation that she lied. And she was quite upset at the notion that her health wasn't restored. Why would she worry them about cancer when she was cured? And she hadn't mentioned Sven until she knew his feelings about the Florida proposal. The day she was planning to call George and Priscilla was the day their shocking letter arrived.

Claudia had interjected herself and hadn't called Elli first to learn Elli's thoughts on the matter. This infuriated Elli. Claudia, not even proposing a suitable option for George and Priscilla, had destroyed the option for Elli. Perhaps that anger was one that Elli harbored.

*   *   *   *   *

After the issue between my sisters was quietly on the back burner my second husband, Lou, visited Claudia with me. Naturally Claudia hadn't come to our wedding, and he was curious to meet my artistic renegade sister. Lou and Claudia shared appreciations of excesses and extravagances. He didn't blink at always being the one to pick up the tab, and had no objections to finishing another bottle of wine. In addition to complimenting her artistic talents, he proved his sincerity by buying paintings from her. Lou, of French heritage, was jovial and known for his loud, exaggerated laughter. Claudia favored anything

French. Lou was a man who gave her bear hugs and affectionately petted her new little poodle, Princess, in his lap. Claudia adored him.

Lou was a podiatrist. The only mistake he made with Claudia was to notice her feet and say, "Ah, you have the same feet and bunions as Elli."

Claudia immediately reprimanded him with, "Never make any comparison or mention of Elli when you're referring to me. We're entirely different. I have no interest whatsoever in talking about Elli. If you want to keep me happy, leave her out of it."

Lou was momentarily stunned but took Claudia at her word. He never mentioned Elli in conversations with Claudia. Lou was also sympathetic that Claudia seemed to have such an uphill struggle in attaining buyers for her artwork. He thought we, meaning me, should help her with that. Claudia liked the idea of my being her Midwest agent.

The majority of Claudia's paintings at that time were of four main theme categories: African animals, motivated by her experiences while painting the murals at the Kenya Safari Club, full-canvas greatly enlarged flower centers, Mexican street scenes, and seascapes. She also had a number of French or Italian charming street scenes most of which were in her private collection, thereby not for sale unless they were accompanied with all of the complications of "second studies."

My attempts at being an agent and helping represent Claudia the artist for the next couple of years provided a series of miseries for our relationship. We had the tedious job of establishing a list of paintings with their titles and dimensions. Getting Claudia to establish a price list was quite an obstacle. Painting by painting she'd make the points of how long the painting had taken to complete, the brushstrokes and details that were in it, the cost of the frame she'd chosen, and thereby the difference in price if the client preferred it unframed. In some cases she'd go through all that explanation and then say, "But this one is part of my private collection. This one isn't for sale. If you find a buyer for this, tell them I'll do a second study, either smaller or larger."

Eventually I asked her not to include photos of her private collection among the ones she wanted me to market. Claudia's reticence to assigning prices to the ones she was willing to sell was a true test of patience for me.

She was also skeptical about consigning any paintings to galleries because a gallery showing her work had punctured one of her paintings. Had I lived in Carmel the job would have been difficult enough. But living halfway across the country, marketing from photographs, and calculating shipping and insurance was a nightmare. I was the founder, owner, business manager and primary teacher at my dance studio where I also co-directed a student performing group and a liturgical dance company, combined with my roles as wife and mother. Claudia gave no considerations to those priorities in my life.

Claudia, not trusting my knowledge and instincts with Milwaukee gallery owners and contacts, came to Milwaukee for me to introduce her to my local possibilities. Though to me she clarified that pricing to galleries was double the amount I would quote to personal friends, Claudia told me simply to introduce her and then watch and listen to her to learn how to deal with galleries. In that process I agonized as I observed her same reticence to declare prices, a test of patience to the gallery managers. The same thing happened with several friends of mine who were interested in her paintings.

Because Claudia's African animal collection was exceptional, I arranged a meeting with the director of Milwaukee's Zoological Society that had a special event coming up. Her work would have been perfect for their event and would have given her excellent exposure. Again Claudia's willingness to describe her painting process, and inability to get down to brass tacks, closed the door on that possibility.

Though a couple of gallery friends loved Claudia's work and had potential clients, they worked on a consignment rather than outright purchase basis. Claudia simply wouldn't give me a free hand in negotiating.

My friends would say complimentary things such as, "You do such beautiful work."

Claudia would ask if they were drawn to any painting in particular. A friend would scramble again through the photos and say, "I love this one, but I have no suitable place for it in my house."

Claudia would say, "If you love it you should have it."

My friend would say, "What kind of price do you set on a painting like this?"

"Ah," Claudia would respond, "That was a particularly difficult painting." She'd detail the difficulties, the time the painting took, various accompanying stories.

My friend would say, "It is beautiful. How much would it cost me?"

Claudia would go on, "If you love it, price isn't a problem. I could take payments over a period of time, whatever period you might need, and then I could send the painting to you."

My friend might go on, "Well, I'll write down the dimensions and see if there is a place it might work in my home, but I'll have to tell my husband how much it will set us back."

Conversations like this would drive me crazy. My friends would be as polite and delicate as they could in their search for the bottom line. Claudia seemed to be assessing whether her work was sufficiently valued, whether her work was going to an appreciative home, what other of her paintings might be of interest to the potential purchaser, and what kind of sales story she and they might have for the telling in years to come. She nonetheless considered my position as agent foremost without a thought of the other ongoing priorities in my life.

In private conversations I had with Claudia in my attempts to learn more of her sales history, I primarily learned of trades she had made of her artworks. She traded for dental work. She traded for a facelift. Most of her sales were commissioned works, not something already in her collection.

Lou and I had two dinner parties to introduce Claudia to groups of our friends. Beforehand, Claudia checked our refrigerator and asked if we had enough wine for the group. I assured her that our basement refrigerator was well stocked. It did surprise me however, that she had her first glass of wine mid-morning and kept refilling her glass during the day.

At dinner, it apparently bothered Claudia that several conversations were going at the same time. She tapped her knife on the side of her wine glass and repeated, "Excuse me" until she had everyone's attention. She suggested that we have a full-group conversation. She'd chosen a topic. Explaining that she always found it challenging to get gifts for men, she requested that each person around the table tell their suggestions of gifts for men. Dutifully our guests answered the question. Generally they disagreed with Claudia's position that choosing gifts for men was difficult. As soon as the round was complete, they resumed the multiple conversations that had been disrupted.

Combined with her daytime drinking, Claudia's dinner drinks had her slurring non-sequiturs. Lou and I later noted to each other that we'd never experienced such a quick exit of guests. The exodus occurred as soon as dinner was over. I wondered how often Claudia's desire to be the center of attention went awry as it had that evening.

The same pattern accompanied our next dinner party for Claudia. She started drinking even earlier that day. The knife on the wine glass clinked again though I don't recall the subject she chose that night. A couple of our friends took to the subject and dominated it. After dessert, rather than suggesting that we retire to the living room for after-dinner drinks, we offered them at the dining table. Claudia was no longer trying to outwit the other talkers. Our guests were staying longer, and Claudia was silently having one glass of Cointreau after another.

Eventually guests excused themselves to return to their homes. Charlie, a favorite friend of ours, joined us with Claudia in the living room. Charlie focused his attention on Claudia asking her questions about her perspectives and experiences. She was un-cooperative. Her answers were terse, very slurred terse. Finally she said, "Well, if you'd just go home, I could go to bed."

Charlie protested that she could go to bed anyway, that he hadn't been with us for a while and wanted to catch up more with what was going on in our lives. Claudia told him that wasn't considered polite behavior in California, but she did take the opportunity to go to bed. Lou and I complimented our friend for not letting Claudia shoo him out the door. We stayed up and chatted at leisure.

Surprisingly Claudia seemed to have no hangover the morning after either of these parties. She thought we had peculiar friends. After all, they'd been invited in order to meet her, and then they paid more attention to each other. And she thought Charlie was downright rude. Why had he asked all those questions of her when he could see she was tired? And why had we stayed up later with him when he'd been so inconsiderate? Clearly her comments set up a no-win framework for us. Neither defense of our friends nor confrontation of her behavior was going to create any positive results. Escape-avoidance prevailed.

I was amazed by how much alcohol she could consume. That she didn't collapse in toxic shock was astounding for such a petite body.

Her sudden changes of subject also intrigued me. I wondered how many toxins of her art supplies might have produced schisms in her brain. I remembered how often she put the brush in her mouth when she water colored. How many chemicals had she ingested?

Claudia was a more active correspondent and phone-caller during those years when I was trying to make art connections for her. A year or more after the dinner parties Lou even funded my way to spend another week with Claudia in Carmel. By this time I realized that no matter how many fascinating experiences, perspectives and pleasures she could share with me, I would pay the price, figuratively and often literally. On a personal basis I experienced what I called the tap test: a torture system where you'd be tapped lightly on your collarbone. The tapping would continue rhythmically like a baton or a slowly dripping faucet on the same spot until it was raw. Then, dreading the next tap, you'd think you might lessen the pain by anticipating it. The distraction of awaiting the next tap severely compromised any substantive participation in ongoing circumstances.

Claudia's application of these figurative taps usually occurred in a string of smaller and larger personal criticisms at any time or in any circumstance. My personal grooming, my contributions to my children's faults, my interests, my friends, my abuses of fashion, my choices of foods, my rampant curiosity, my ideas, perspectives, behavior and place in the world were all tap targets. Clearly my own psychological states, of being the vulnerable and sibling-abused child or the innocent Cinderella subject to the entitlements of her sisters, made the tap system totally accessible to Claudia. Super-sensitivity and vulnerability was not my stance and nature with the rest of the world. Nonetheless it was immediately on tap with Claudia. It was predictable, predictable in the same way that any phone call from Claudia was accompanied by some assignment, some request, some required action that needed to be prioritized to the top of any "To Do" list.

Even when I developed conscious awareness of my role in the tap system, my childhood position all too easily came into play. The capable, self-confident, problem-solving person I was accustomed to being as an adult would disappear at less than a moment's notice. There would be some lapse in sequence, some sudden zap, some defensive squirt of adrenaline that would have me floundering.

Though the tap test was more dangerous on a face-to-face basis, I traveled out to Carmel again. On this particular visit with Claudia, the accumulations of the tap test reached a new depth in my own psyche. Claudia and I were still at the breakfast table as she developed the litany of what was or wasn't allowed in my being her art agent. Rapidly, volume and emotions crescendoed into a shouting-sobbing match between the two of us.

Claudia asserted how I didn't understand art and the life of an artist, how I didn't understand sales and marketing. With tears rolling down her face she screamed at me how her paintings were her babies, how they'd been created with love and joy and needed to be in loving homes with people who appreciated them. It was my lack of understanding and my ineptitude that was the failure in our attempt to work together as artist and agent.

With tears streaming down my face I screamed back at her. My sense of it as it was happening was one of an out-of-body experience. I could see myself as my own body and voice, but as an unrecognizable personality, as if I were watching a movie rather than really being there. My screaming was lambasting her with point after point. I shouted that the recognition and respect she expected in the sales process was unrealistic. If she wanted to sell paintings she'd better start painting them to be sold. If a person loved her painting that didn't mean it fit into their home. People weren't going to redecorate a room to accommodate a painting's color scheme or content. They weren't going to buy a bigger house to accommodate a painting that was too big for their space. If she kept seeing her paintings as her babies, that was why she couldn't put a price on them or sell them. She was allowing herself a framework that was tantamount to selling her babies. I reminded her that our nephew and his wife had visited her and would love to have a painting or two of hers. She told them no prices so they didn't know if their favorites were in their budgetary range. I shouted that she loved her own paintings more than anyone else could love them. She wasn't painting them to sell them. She only traded the ones she wasn't as enthusiastic about for services she felt improved her own appearance, her dental work and her face-lift. The only paintings she was happy to sell were commissions, ones she had pre-agreed to sell before she even started them. The small gallery space she rented for about a year in Carmel was a failure because nearly all of the paintings she had there were her personal collection, not for sale. Tourists and art collectors who came to Carmel didn't want to wait or risk her offers of doing second studies. People didn't like to make a financial commitment when they didn't know if her second studies would please them as much as the originals.

Claudia stood up. She took our argumentative exchange in the direction of philosophy and Eastern religion. She screamed at me to "Come Up," to find true beauty and joy. For me the circumstances were far from my achieving a state of spiritual enlightenment. That she expected me to "come up" in the midst of the verbal battery going on between us astounded me. Instead I realized how pathetic we were. She was right; there was a lot I didn't understand. I in turn had disregarded the potential for injury in what I'd said to her. I felt ashamed of that. I walked around the table and hugged her. She hugged me back as we both stood there and wept until we could breathe again. No more emotional storms arose that day.

Surprisingly, the next day she asked me which paintings our nephew and his wife had loved. I didn't know the answer. Before I flew back to Milwaukee I bought a small painting of poppies from her. She gave me another painting of the same size, one of Monet's garden, saying that she thought it would be a good pairing with the poppies, and that it was a gift.

During summers Claudia would have private students and friends who wanted to expand their knowledge of painting techniques come to her house for classes. Despite her money woes she also managed to take an occasional trip. Victoria and another friend went with her to Paris. They discovered that they weren't well-suited as traveling companions, so Claudia traveled on alone to Italy. She met various people who were attractive to her and had adventures that were worth the rift with Victoria. She casually knit-in the benefits of room-rate reductions or free dinners attained through successful seductions.

Later she took a solo trip to England. When she got home she called. Her big announcement was that she was in love. She said she would marry this man in a heartbeat and live-happily-ever-after. Claudia hadn't spoken about this potential direction of her life in a long time. She was certain that she had encountered "The" man on her trip.

It turned out that he was not an Englishman but an oilman from Texas. As I pressed her for details, I was disheartened to learn that she had met him at the bar in an elegant hotel in which she'd elected to stay.

They had a number of drinks and she'd rapturously stayed the night with him in his room. But she was in love, completely in love. Though he'd left the next day on a business trip, and she took her scheduled flight back home, he'd promised that he was soon coming to visit her at her home in California. He was blown away by what an exceptional person she was and by the photographs of her wonderful artworks. He said he'd visit her within two weeks. This was "The" man.

A few days later she called to tell me that she had called his Texas office and obtained the number to reach him at a business conference in London. She called him collect to read him a love poem and to learn the dates he was coming to see her. He was delighted to hear from her and heady with the poem, but said he'd be delayed in getting to California because a series of European conferences required his presence.

Claudia called me a number of times with updates including his repeated postponements of plans to visit her. She was thriving on being in love, but would also say, "I must be crazy. How can I live with an oil man when I'm an environmentalist?"

The time came when her collect calls no longer got through to him. No responses or updates came from him. That was that. As Claudia said, whatever made her think that she could tolerate a life with an oilman. It wasn't meant to be.

Deaths/Decades/Reversals/Revisions

After the terrible prior gathering of sisters in Carmel, and Elli's subsequent trip, and the squelching of plans with Uncle George and Aunt Priscilla, Elli and Claudia simply stayed out of each other's hair. My relationship with Elli was a great counterbalance to the continuum of dilemmas Claudia presented. Forthright and trusting, Elli and I shared our news, perspectives and ideas openly.

Unfortunately after a few years of feeling cancer-free, Elli learned that her cancer had metastasized into bone cancer. Disenchanted with western medicine, and encouraged by Sven, Elli sought herbal and natural solutions. She decided to beat the cancer with diet. Elements of the diet were no red meats, lots of fresh fruits and vegetables, no milk or milk products except butter, no fried foods or canned foods, purified water, lots of seeds and nuts and vitamin supplements.

Claudia agreed with Elli's choice of a natural recovery. Claudia avoided doctors, other than dentists and plastic surgeons. Claudia also read extensively about the chemical content of foods and what combinations of foods produced the best combinations of needed vitamins and iron. Claudia was also particularly well-versed about salves and lotions that had anti-wrinkle or anti-aging qualities.

Elli's diet worked. Within a few months her bone cancer was completely in remission to the point of being no longer detectible. Six seemingly cancer-free years passed before Elli, then age sixty, developed liver cancer. Learning of a supposedly successful treatment center in Mexico, Elli, with financial help from Mother, went there.

Although Elli and Claudia thought they had irresolvable differences and that seeking solutions was a waste of time, when Elli's liver cancer progressed, Claudia became an active support system by writing or calling Elli daily. Elli and I were taking turns at daily phone calls. Claudia would call me a couple times weekly noting that the situation

44

with Elli was dangerous, that Elli carried far too much anger that was the cause of her cancer, and that we had to train Elli to think positively so that she could survive this ordeal.

Despite Claudia's good intentions, Elli didn't want to be in communication with Claudia or with Mother. Sven was staying with Elli as much as his chiropractic business would allow. He screened phone calls to accommodate Elli's wishes to avoid Claudia's calls.

Whether anger was the cause of Elli's cancer, Claudia proved to be correct that Elli carried a lot of anger. Elli had never overcome the rage she held about many debilitating aspects and abusive episodes from her prior marriage. References to that surfaced frequently as her cancer progressed. Elli was also furious that cancer was spoiling this point in her life when she had a happy and supportive relationship with Sven, and when she had four darling grandchildren she adored. Another unfortunate concept she embraced from Claudia's letters was a vengeance toward Mother. To vent that anger Elli wrote a series of rage-filled, blaming and cruel letters to Mother. My attempts to counsel or contain Elli or Claudia about this were ineffective. Other than normal irritations and annoyances between parent and child, I'd always had a positive and caring relationship with Mother. Unfortunately, Claudia and Elli blamed Mother for any unpleasant elements in their lives. I couldn't imagine what my sisters had experienced prior to my birth that made them so vengeful.

Elli, with her extraordinary strong will to live, survived the liver cancer for a year and a quarter. I spent three separate two-week periods with her during that time. She died on what would have been my father's birthday. Claudia didn't come to the funeral nor did she want a copy of the primary eulogy I delivered at it.

I found it heart-wrenching that Claudia's vengeance and vicious letters to Mother continued. Had Claudia known that Mother herself would be gone within a year, it probably wouldn't have made a difference. Perhaps Elli's loss to cancer and Claudia's associated thesis of rage provoked her behavior. Interestingly though, Claudia still practiced philosophical guidance from her studies of Eastern religions and her years of belonging to the Vedanta Society. Claudia started attending Science of Mind services. There were many parallels between it and the Christian Science background in which Mother had been raised.

Though Mother continued as a Deacon of the Presbyterian Church where she had run the nursery school for twenty-five years, her internalized practice of Christian Science was strongly encouraged to resurface by Clarence. He had never left his Christian Science rearing. So Mother and Claudia held compatible beliefs on healing powers and the value of daily readings.

Clarence conveyed clearly that Mother was too quick to contribute financially to her daughters all of whom he thought lived extravagantly. He had made the one exception of contributing half of the ten thousand dollars they had given Elli for her cancer treatment in Mexico. He was vigilant in preventing Mother from making any further contributions of significance to Claudia.

For many reasons all of us had problems with the boring, tedious, controlling presence of Clarence in Mother's life. Clarence had been a boyfriend of hers in college. She found him well-mannered and attentive, but she loved the other couple with whom they always double-dated. Clarence by himself bored her. She had enjoyed his clear adoration and that he was a tall, handsome, mannerly man. But he offered no ideas, insights, wit or humor. The rugged manliness of our dad with his analytical mind, his range of interests, his clever humor and his equal adoration of Mother had quickly eliminated Clarence from her field of suitors.

Clarence said he'd always kept track of Mother through college newsletters because she had always been his true love. He was a retired professor of drafting. Clarence didn't drink, smoke or swear. He was a suit-and-tie man who declared ad-infinitum that everything about Mother was beautiful and adorable, and that all of her many activities were worthy and admirable. He was willing for her to keep her home, activities and broad circle of friends. He would keep his home too, and they would travel every few weeks between the two. She would do all the driving because he was no longer comfortable behind the wheel. They could still have a long and happy life together because his objective was to live to be a hundred.

Claudia said the reason Mother had married him was that it made such a good story for Mother to tell of the late-in-life smitten suitor finally tracking down his Cinderella. The details and developments of their relationship were less glamorous. Claudia's only in-person experience was during the several days they stayed with her in Carmel about a year after they were married. Claudia's assessment was that Mother was thriving on his relentless adoration, but that there was something basically evil about Clarence. His lurking evilness presented itself to her in several daydreams and nightmares she had after their visit. She certainly was glad to have him out of her house. His constant turning to Claudia and seeking affirmation of his question, "Isn't she wonderful" had driven her nuts.

Clarence drove us all crazy with that one. There were only so many times you could answer, "Yes, she's wonderful" before you wanted to rant, "No, she makes mistakes and has faults just like the rest of us." It wasn't long before Mother herself felt smothered by him. Occasionally she was assertive in shooting biting comments in his direction. Her addiction to his adoration, however, trumped all countermeasures.

For the rest of us, Clarence's ambition to reach a hundred was a miserable prospect. Mother's sudden death from arteriosclerosis in the fifteenth year of their marriage betrayed our hopes that she would at least outlive him.

Rather than being contacted by Clarence, I got the call from my childhood friend who was visiting her mom across the street from my Indiana home. She said she had just seen the paramedics take my mom to the hospital. I made a few calls to cover my obligations at the studio and home, threw some clothes in a suitcase and raced to my hometown. I went directly to the hospital only to learn that I was too late. After a brief time of stunned and helpless silence next to Mother's dead body, I drove on to the house.

Clarence, sitting by himself in the living room, was surprised to see me walk in. He sobbed, "Dorothy is gone. I've lost my Dorothy." I asked if he'd been trying to call me. He said, "No. I just can't believe it. Dorothy's gone. I've lost my Dorothy." And he sobbed some more.

Eventually Clarence told me the story of her sudden collapse. I called Lou to give him the report. I called my son Clarke who was in Philly. My older son Zak was out of the country. I called Elli's kids. I called Claudia. Claudia said she wasn't surprised, that with Clarence's hovering Mother hadn't been taking good care of herself for quite some time.

I called Carrie, my childhood friend, who came across the street to talk with me. After Clarence said that he planned to handle all the funeral arrangements, we finally convinced him to go to bed.

The details of that experience would make a book in itself. Every element was difficult, and coping with Clarence was horrendous. I needed Claudia to be a fully participating sister. Her response was that whatever I decided was fine. There wasn't anything from the house that she wanted except for me to keep the paintings she'd made for Mother. She'd definitely not come back for the funeral. She hoped never to see our hometown again. She was staying focused on searching for a bigger house for herself in the Carmel area.

Though I had no phone privacy because Clarence always stood nearby or listened in, I continued to call Claudia with updates. They were minimized not only because of Clarence's presence but because of Claudia's lack of interest. Her descriptions of houses she was looking at, the pros and cons of them, her financial potential to afford or not afford them, only frustrated me and added to my misery.

Clarence's only surviving niece had a limo drive her along with her church's minister from middle Illinois to Mother's funeral service. She told me what a charming and capable woman my mother was and that she'd never been able to understand how Mother had been able to tolerate Clarence that long. Clarence's niece steered herself away from Clarence at every opportunity. Had he ever recognized her disdain for him he might not have so instantly changed his will to leave everything to her. This niece, already rolling in dough, inherited yet another fortune six months later when Clarence died. His darling Dorothy's daughters received not one penny from Clarence.

Claudia's plans for purchasing a bigger house fell through. In fact the real disaster was that a nasty storm in Carmel caused a large California pine to fall through the charming Casa Claudia. She called me in the middle of the night in a state of terror saying, "A tree just fell through my house. I could have been killed. It's a huge tree. It crashed right through my bedroom ceiling. It landed just past the foot of my bed. It's a huge tree. I could have been killed. The roof and the ceiling are split open. Rain is pouring through the split."

I further learned that the police were there, that she had to leave the house and would spend the remainder of the night at her neighbors.

Not any of Claudia's paintings were damaged by the fallen tree. Claudia had immediately available to her a charming place owned by a friend who was out of the country. She lived there while repairs were made. Her frequent phone calls were full of commentary on damage assessments, insurance claims, considerations of suing the neighbor whose tree had fallen, recommendations and interviews with architects on her new plans. She'd decided to add an interior stairwell and a second-floor studio-gallery above the master bedroom as part of the reconstruction as well as other changes. This of course added complications to how much her insurance company would cover. The number of phone calls and their content gave me the uncomfortable feeling that I was being treated as her substitute mother.

She chose an older architect famous for several other homes in the Carmel area. All conversations from my perspective were disjointed bits and pieces, always coupled with some assignment for Lou and me to research for some other portion of information she needed. Each call also included her exclamation, "I could have been killed." Her wine consumption was obviously on the rise at this time as evidenced by her increasingly slurred speech.

Eventually she had some major squabble with her architect and found a young replacement. This man was married and had a three-year-old child. Claudia nonetheless found him attractive and was sure he was in love with her. He reminded her greatly of our brother Brett. She often had him sit down to lunch with her.

As her architectural plans and rebuilding proceeded, it proved to require the entire inheritance Mother left to her. She kept a steady pressure on me to get Mother's separate estate settled and the money to her. It turned out to time perfectly with the building stages and completion of her house. Her sense of budgeting was at the opposite pole of mine. I was stunned that she spent it all and left herself no financial comfort zone.

Finally she returned to her rebuilt and expanded house. In the distance from a small window in her second floor studio she could see the sea. This pleased her enormously. She loved pouring herself another glass of wine and watching the sunset. She also bought a very expensive 18th century large French armoire for her bedroom. She was pleased that the antique dealer allowed her to make time payments, but regularly complained of being in a financial bind. She also complained about the unreasonable expectations of the staff that continually flared up at the parochial girls' school where she taught art.

As these expenses and problems mounted, she next reported a blessing who arrived at her door one day when she was particularly miserable. She said her doorbell rang, and though she'd just stepped out of the shower and wrapped herself in a towel, she answered the door. It was a man who wanted to know if she wanted to sell all that wood that was stacked along her outer fence.

"Just take it," she told him. "I don't need it. Just take it."

He was taken aback by this woman wrapped in a towel. He asked, "Are you alright?"

She started to cry and sobbed, "I just have too much to deal with."

He stepped in the door, embraced her, and told her he guessed he was sent to comfort her. To her he was indeed the angel sent for that purpose, and she was a willing partner in the rescue. By the time she told me this story he was a regular part of her life. I learned that he was Italian and an excellent cook. She'd never been fond of pasta before, but he made delicious and excellent meals of it for her. He was also a superb lover and sexual pleasure. She'd also given him one of her sculptures that he particularly liked. No matter what distressed her in her life, he assured her that everything would be okay.

As time went on she learned that he had two teenage kids from his former marriage. His obligations to them meant there were times he couldn't be with her. The firewood and other odd jobs were what he was doing until he had his former business license restored. He wore an ankle bracelet so the police could always find him as he was serving a time-release sentence for a conviction in which he'd been framed in his prior business. She said, "The details are unimportant."

Either her calls to him became too frequent or demanding, or his considerations of how to work his kids into the equation became too complex. I don't recall whether that took four months or six, but she was more than confused and unhappy that the relationship ended.

About then she asked me about the separate fifteen thousand dollars of H-bonds we'd each inherited from Mother's estate. Since each of us had been co-listed with Mother on our respective bonds, Claudia thought they should be re-registered. Before I could tell her that I had listed Zak on half and Clarke on half of my bonds, she proposed that she and I list each other. Her response to what I had done was an accusatory question. "You mean that if I co-list you on mine, you're not going to list me on yours?"

She wasn't happy with my answer. I tried to justify it on the mother-child framework. She objected. I went on to say that if she had children

I wouldn't expect her to list me rather than her children. She jumped in that I'd made her point. Without children she didn't have that option, so my converting to her plan was the only fair thing to do. She managed to work in quite a run on the tap test in comments about my sons.

Perhaps three or four days of phone calls were reruns on this issue. I didn't give in. She inserted various interpretations of "didn't I say I loved her?" and hadn't she saved my life when I went through my first divorce?

I eventually said I had no interest in further discussions of the bonds. Her answer was that I didn't love her and that I had no appreciation for all she had done for me. She escalated into screaming. Her final statements were, "I disinherit you. I never want to speak to you again. Don't write. Don't call. If you write I'll throw them out unopened. We're done. I never want to hear from you again. I wish you well, but we're done." She hung up the phone.

I waited for several days expecting it to be Claudia each time the phone rang. By week's end I realized that my sense of shock and mourning was ridiculous. I had always looked for her to be a sister to me. I was glad to no longer be a part of the pre-determined punishment her spirit suffered by being born into our family. I was relieved. I became comfortably content with being disinherited.

$$* \quad * \quad * \quad * \quad *$$

Rather than simply being able to enjoy those years of Claudia's silence, my own "To Do" list at home went through several cycles of misery. Lou sold his business in our commercial building that also housed my studio. This sale required taking a portion of my studio space. Lou also traded other property he owned for another commercial property located away from the area where my students lived. Without funds for local relocation I was heartbroken to close my school that I'd run successfully for fifteen years. I was also dismayed in the course of these commercial transactions to experience the Captain Ahab aspects of Lou.

With my college degree and lifetime teaching certificate I worked the next two years teaching in Milwaukee middle schools. Despite my successes in the classroom, the chaos between school administration and the union weighed heavily on everyone. That prompted me to move to a new career as a travel agent and Master Cruise Counsellor.

Three years had passed since Claudia had disinherited me. Her phone call at that point caught me totally off-guard. No mention was made about the disinheritance or the silent interim. Claudia said she'd been thinking about Aunt Priscilla and Uncle George and wanted to know if I had any update. I shared what I knew. Priscilla and George had moved to a graduated care condo-complex in Naples. George, who hated being old, especially when he could no longer go fishing, lasted a few years and finally achieved the blessing of death. Priscilla became limited to a wheelchair and reported being visited nearly daily by a woman named Zita. Zita had an old vegetative-state relative she visited in the complex. She'd met Priscilla somewhere in that process and preferred Priscilla's animated company. I made the mistake of telling Claudia that I was a travel agent and was completing my Cruise Counsellor certification by doing ship inspections in Florida the next weekend. Claudia said that news was a godsend. She insisted that I rebook my tickets to extend my trip for a day and drive across Florida to visit Priscilla.

The remainder of that week Claudia called me nightly to achieve my agreement to visit Priscilla, to see that I'd spoken with Priscilla to let her know I was coming, to be assured that I'd booked my rental car, to be sure to convey to Priscilla how much and how often Claudia thought of her.

Everything about that trip was difficult. Gale force winds prevailed in the Miami/Ft. Lauderdale areas. Urgent messages arrived from my office alerting me to find some ships in different ports from those scheduled. And finally I did the long drive across state to reach Priscilla's condo only to learn that Priscilla wasn't there. After I'd been misdirected to find her in the condo urgent-care unit, they informed me that she'd been transferred to the hospital. They also said that had a paper on file instructing them not to disclose Priscilla's condition to anyone. Surprisingly the paper was from a law office and signed by Zita as a witness. At the hospital I had to prove I was a relative before they'd let me visit Priscilla.

Priscilla was not the tall willowy blonde I'd remembered. She'd gotten blubbery and looked like a beached walrus in her hospital bed. I had to tell her who I was and show her pictures I'd brought of various family members, including young pictures of Priscilla and George.

Medications perhaps muddled her mind. Nurses had me leave the room several times while they performed various procedures with her.

The fashionable and ebullient Zita arrived, so we were introduced. While Priscilla was fed her lunch, Zita and I lunched together in the hospital cafeteria. I learned that Zita and her husband lived in Wisconsin in the summer months. They spent the rest of the year in Florida where they owned substantial rental properties. They also cruised and traveled abroad extensively. Zita was so glad to have Priscilla to visit since her own relative was comatose. Zita loved Priscilla's active mind and her entertaining stories. She said that Priscilla never overcame mourning the loss of George. I knew that from the way Priscilla became tearful every time he was mentioned.

I told Zita about the paper I'd seen at the urgent care center preventing us from being given reports on Priscilla's condition. I didn't tell her that I'd had them make a photocopy for me. I don't recall what fuzzy story Zita told me about it, but I asked her to contact the attorney and have it removed. Our family was entitled to know what was going on with our aunt. Zita gave me her addresses and phone numbers and said she's keep me updated about Priscilla's condition. She told me that Priscilla had a history of falling and breaking bones. I knew that too from occasional calls I'd made to Priscilla after George's death.

I had more private time with Priscilla after Zita left. Priscilla said she didn't know how long she'd last but she suspected it wouldn't be much longer. Without being specific, she said she needed to change her Will again.

Upon my arrival back in Milwaukee, Claudia was on the phone reaping a full report. She was instantly skeptical about Zita, labeling her a vulture influencing Priscilla who historically drank too much. Claudia felt certain that Zita was positioning herself in order to manipulate Priscilla and inherit her estate. I thought that was unlikely especially since Zita already had more wealth that she knew what to do with. But Claudia's thesis fit with the photocopied paper I brought home.

In short, Priscilla didn't last many months longer. Zita called to notify me of Priscilla's death. Priscilla had informed her lawyer of her wishes to be carried out when she died. There was to be no funeral or memorial service. Within a week the Will came. It left five thousand dollars each to Claudia, to me, and to our cousin. The rest of the nearly three-quarter million estate was left to Zita, and all Priscilla's household furnishings and personal effects were left to a Korean friend of hers.

It looked as if Claudia's assessment of Zita was correct. Claudia then pressed me to contact a former Milwaukee lawyer relocated in Miami Beach. Claudia was adamant that we should not be boondoggled out of our rights as next of kin. After my lawyer friend did research in depth as a huge favor, blow-by-blow accounts were shared with Claudia. It turned out that Priscilla had made various changes to her Will seven times since George's death. We could go to court to contest her last Will as next-of-kin rightful inheritors. If we won on the most current Will, we would then need to repeat and win the court procedures six more times to get back to the Will that divided the estate equally between the next-of-kin. Seven times in court would eat up the majority of the estate's value for which we'd be "out of pocket" in the interim. This would take years, with no assured victory, and leave us financially about where we were in Priscilla's last Will. In short, Zita walked away with the estate in hand. That brought George and Priscilla's chapter to a close. Many aspects of it would come to mind later in ways we would never have anticipated.

More calls came over time bringing back the typical format of our relationship before I'd been disinherited. Eventually she conveyed that the parochial school had finally let her go. She no longer had employment. I figured her drinking had contributed to her job loss. She was on the classic path of an alcoholic. She admitted to having a drinking problem but rejected the label of alcoholic.

My role was that of listener. I tried to convey the concept and process of reciprocity to her. My observation was that reciprocity was something she bypassed in her relationships. One friend after another of hers got cast aside. They would disappoint her in some unforgivable way and she would be done with them. Disinheritance was not limited to me, nor was her abandonment of friends who didn't buy or continue to buy her artwork.

If I shared my perspective or made a suggestion, Claudia would tell me I was wrong, and balk, "I didn't ask you for any advice. I just need to vent. I just need to get these things off my chest. I feel this pressure in my chest. This stress is unhealthy. I need to be able to vent to you."

I was skeptical. She had no conscious awareness of how demanding and demeaning she was. She was clear that she wanted to be the center of attention. She was clear that other people paled by comparison with her own range of experiences and studies. By squelching niceties such as reciprocity, fair sharing, equal time, she could retain her show-stopping position in center ring. By intentionally minimizing others she probably felt she was benevolently giving them the gift of her own fascinating self and her exceptional talents. That fit Elli's assertion that Claudia built a stone-wall, fortifying herself against any external influence and assuring herself of an unchallenged position in center ring.

A new person in Claudia's life who had no objection to her holding center ring was Edgar, an older gentleman she'd met on one of her regular visits to the library. He was a widower whose eyesight no longer allowed him to read. He was looking for someone to read to him.

They established a weekly pattern of his taking her to lunch so he would have some companionship in exchange for her reading an hour or so to him. As weeks passed pleasantly this way, he reached the point of asking to kiss her.

"No. No," she said, as she tick-tocked her finger in front of him. "No kisses. No romance. That's not part of our arrangement." Week after week Edgar persisted in this further request, as Claudia persisted in her, "No. No."

She enjoyed his company, the lunches and the reading but wasn't interested in the prospect of taking care of an old man. Even when he met another woman, also named Claudia, who agreed to occasional kisses, our Claudia held to her rules.

Edgar then started talking of leaving an inheritance to his other Claudia. Our Claudia didn't mind Edgar's directing his desire for kisses and perhaps more, elsewhere. But she did let him know that she had no objections to being an inheritor. She also advised him that leaving more to the people he loved more was only sensible.

Tidbits of reading and lunches with Edgar were conveyed only when I'd ask about him. Eventually setbacks to his health brought their lunch pattern to a close. When he died our Claudia was named as an inheritor. She received five thousand dollars. She wondered what the other Claudia inherited.

*   *   *   *   *

In the next few years my sons both came back into play for Claudia. Claudia decided to research and approach Philadelphia art galleries.

Clarke and his wife, Daphne, still dancing with the Pennsylvania Ballet, responded yes to Claudia's request to stay with them while she was on this mission. Ever since Clarke had decided to become a professional dancer, Claudia determined that he was the other artistic spirit in the family, the one who was kindred to her. Claudia additionally appreciated that Clarke and Daphne were also dog-lovers with their beautiful Samoyed. Daphne was bursting with curiosity having never met Clarke's infamous aunt. Claudia, of course, hadn't attended their wedding, though she did ship them a large painting of giraffes dancing in the clouds.

Clarke's demeanor as he gave account of the visit sounded like a child being tickled. Claudia's behavior, her gallery visits, her comments, everything, was just bizarre and amusing to Clarke. Daphne's report was that Claudia treated Daphne as an invisible person married to a god. Daphne said that Claudia idolized Clarke, that he could do no wrong, and that everything he said and did was wonderful. Daphne was fascinated by being so completely unnoticed. This was a new experience for her.

Claudia's report of her visit was that Clarke was "such a darling." He had tended to her every need and was just a joy. Claudia didn't know what to think of Daphne and admitted that she hadn't taken much notice of her. She did take notice that their apartment was a small space to share with a large dog, and that Clarke and Daphne couldn't afford to splurge much. Claudia's research on Philadelphia art galleries was disappointing. She decided it wasn't a suitable market for her artwork.

By that time Lou and I had done a Starker Exchange by trading our prior office/studio building for a vacation home in Santa Fe. That unloaded the sad reminder of closing the studio, and it presented the future possibility of a home for our eventual retirement. Unintentionally on our part, it also captured Claudia's interest.

Claudia's call was enthusiastic about her desire to explore the Santa Fe market. She decided that its additional benefit was in being within driving distance of Carmel. By then Zak was working in Santa Fe and living in our vacation home. Claudia was eager for me to arrange for her to stay five days with Zak. In retrospect I could have opted for another round of disinheritance. Instead, I apologized to Zak and made the arrangements. Internally I couldn't dodge knowing that it would be a test of tolerance for both of them.

After her visit Claudia reported that there was an overabundance of mediocre southwestern art in Santa Fe, but that she had found a few galleries that were possibilities for her. She noted that there was a high level of wealth in the area and there were plenty of fashionably dressed and bejeweled tourists who would constitute a good market for her artworks. She found that Zak even with his world experiences and double master's degrees had made no advances in manners. She didn't understand why he usually cooked at home when Santa Fe restaurants were plentiful and excellent. He also obviously preferred beer to wine, so it was fortunate that she'd brought her own supply. She observed that Zak seemed to have exceptionally long work hours and that she would have enjoyed a bit more companionship while she was there.

Zak reported that Claudia was failing physically, that she walked very slowly and panted with the slightest bit of exertion. He wondered every day if she'd make it back up the hill of Canyon Road. He said that she drank herself into oblivion on a daily basis. He thought she'd had some pretty nasty experiences in the galleries. She told him that one gallery owner shouted her out of his gallery and was so upset that he continued shouting until she'd gotten out of his entry courtyard. Apparently she was asked to leave another gallery because she was showing her artwork photographs to customers.

That description exemplified absence of boundaries as another element of Claudia's personality. She was often aghast at what offensive statements people made to her without her awareness that her own out-of-bounds entitlements may have prompted their behavior.

Having abandoned my wish for a calm compatible sisterly relationship, I continued to search for clues to understanding her. Though Mother may have set the stage in Claudia's early years for her to be the remarkable performer, Mother's Christian Science or elements of her own personality probably contributed to absence of diagnosis of a personality disorder. Psychology books note that personality disorders often were hidden by more obvious behavior problems, frequently alcoholism.

Over the years Lou bought a number of her large flower paintings to decorate his new office. Then came a Christmas that he enthusiastically gave me a surprise gift, a large painting he'd bought from Claudia. He'd promised we would hang it over our living room fireplace.

Claudia called to ask if I'd opened all my presents yet. That year Claudia had made her first journey to paint in Monet's garden, a subject that dominated her primary artworks for years thereafter. She told me how the painting Lou had selected was her very best one and how difficult it had been to paint. She wanted to know if I loved it and how it looked in the living room.

Lou had put the painting above the fireplace immediately, replacing another of Claudia's paintings that I'd loved there for years. Although I felt the colors in the new painting were out of context with the rest of the room, I told Claudia that I loved it and that it made a remarkable difference in the room. I told Lou what a thoughtful and generous gift it was and how totally delighted Claudia was that he'd gotten it for me. I'd lied to both of them. My statements were half-truths at best.

That painting held its featured place in the living room beyond the remainder of my marriage with Lou. Lou's Ahab factors, not the painting, led to our divorce. In the division of property, despite my encouragement, he chose not to take the painting. Claudia was sad to lose his patronage.

Delighted/Distraught/Determined

Though wary of men and marriage, and resigned to completing my life solo, there was a surprise in store for me. Despite my resistance, I was being courted by a man who just wouldn't go away and who gave me boosts of a hundred hilarious moments. With my friends saying they were glad to hear me laughing again and they'd never seen me happier, Paolo took his place in my life. And I gained a whole new zany Italian family along with him. He was entertaining and helpful in myriad ways to anyone and everyone, even Claudia whom he met by telephone. They happily chatted for nearly two years of calls before they met face to face.

I was involved in the difficult obstacle course of selling the house in Santa Fe when Paolo ran into his first conflict with Claudia. Paolo realized how Claudia was distressing me with tales of episodes in her life when I was pressed with resolving many issues in my own. Because I was distracted by arrangements and negotiations on the Santa Fe house, Claudia was chastising me for being inattentive and unsupportive to her. Paolo reprimanded her for that on the next call. On the call after that when Paolo answered, Claudia didn't greet him but immediately said, "I'd like to speak with my sister." This infuriated Paolo who said in a loud voice as he handed the phone to me, "It's your sister. I never want to speak to this woman again."

I think Claudia was as astounded as I was. She knew that Paolo was mannerly and that she had sacrificed her right to be treated in a mannerly way. When Paolo would answer subsequent calls from Claudia, he wouldn't even greet her. He'd simply hand the phone to me.

Claudia eventually apologized to him, and sometimes without even asking to speak with me, just had conversations with him. When she heard that we were going to a business conference in Charleston, she announced that she'd meet us there because she planned to move to Charleston. She no longer had a job to report to in Carmel. She'd also decided that the politics of Carmel and its galleries were disgusting. She'd had enough of Carmel.

Before the Charleston trip she had Paolo do extensive research into real estate in the Charleston area. She took a pre-trip there and made arrangements for a realtor to pick her up at the airport and spend several days showing her properties. She returned to familiarize herself more with Charleston for a day or two before we arrived for our conference. By pre-arrangement with Claudia, at the end of the first afternoon of the conference we met her for an hour at the five-star Charleston Place Hotel. During her prior house shopping she'd learned that this hotel's cocktail lounge with its piano accompanist and its delectable dish of snacks was the best place to have a glass of wine. It was the first face-to-face meeting of Claudia and Paolo. I was pleased to see it going smoothly. Our conversational agenda was to make various rendezvous arrangements for the next few days.

Claudia did one thing at our cocktail hour that Paolo judged "out of bounds." When Claudia tapped on her empty wine glass and said, "Another Chardonnay, Paolo," he dutifully flagged the waitress, noting Claudia's automatic expectation that he would pick up the tab. Coupled with the fact that he and I obviously weren't going to have another round, reaffirmed to him that his framework in any dealings with Claudia needed to be "stay vigilant and proceed with caution".

While Paolo was at conferences the next day, I walked to the lovely French Bed and Breakfast where Claudia was staying. After exploring its charming public rooms and gardens we walked back into town center where I treated her to lunch before we shopped Charleston's antique stores and boutiques. Knowing how I agitated and embarrassed Claudia by trying things on in shops, I avoided trying anything on except a couple beautiful and very expensive high fashion sweater-jackets. Why was I surprised that my perpetually cash-poor sister bought one for herself? Shopping done, I then treated us to one round of her recommended Kendall-Jackson chardonnay at Charleston Place before we joined Paolo at our conference hotel. Paolo treated us to dinner at an elegant Charleston restaurant that Claudia recommended.

When Paolo had the next afternoon free, we picked up Claudia and drove out to Mt Pleasant to look at the house she'd bought. We were skeptical about Claudia's arranging all the sale transactions so quickly. She had followed her game plan to first find a suitable house in Charleston and then have a realtor sell her house in Carmel on a timetable that would meet her contingency for closing. Her brand new house was in a gated community in Mt Pleasant about a half-hour's drive from Charleston. The house was a thirty-five hundred square foot red brick house with a large grassy front and side yard and a boggy back yard. As was true in all of Charleston's surrounding areas, old plantations had been bought and sub-divided into housing developments.

Though Claudia didn't have a key so that we could do an inside tour, we peered in some windows and saw the large open living room with its cathedral windows as well as its fireplace. Replacing a couple cracked windows in the living room and re-grading to eliminate the bog of the back yard was built into her contract along with redoing the brick fascia that was unevenly applied to the two-car garage. These repairs were to be done before Claudia and poodle-Princess moved in.

We were mystified that the back yard was so wet. This seemed out of context with a cotton plantation. Furthermore there was an extensive swamp behind it with cattails, and Claudia commented that an alligator had been spotted in the neighborhood. We noted that there was no roof or cover over the front door, a problem for rainy days. Still, none of us had any idea of what a nightmare this house would cause within a year of her moving into it.

Claudia had arranged for us to meet her realtor and his wife and treat all of us to lunch the next day. The realty couple were pleasing conversationalists and accommodating to each of Claudia's requests and observations including ours about the house. They also informed us that the plantations in that area were rice plantations, not cotton. That explained the bog. Claudia also made the point several times about how happy she was that this lunch was her treat for us. She bought a bottle of wine to accompany the meal. Paolo, thinking in advance, managed to fill each of our glasses to empty the bottle. With his own glass emptied as the meal progressed he turned to Claudia to convey that he thought we needed another bottle of wine. She responded that the rest of us could make the remainder in our glasses suffice, that another bottle wasn't necessary, but that she'd order another glass for him. Thus, Paolo was satisfied that this brought her "another chardonnay, Paolo" into balance.

Upon our return to Milwaukee Claudia's phone calls covered the details of the sale of her Carmel house, the expenses of packing and shipping her paintings, and concerns about the cross-country trip with Princess who hated being in the car. When I declined her request to have the fourteen boxes of sculpture molds shipped for storage at my house, she pursued Clarke to agree despite the space limitations of his living quarters. My own refusal came very close to causing me to be disinherited again.

Her long drive across country was accompanied with delays caused by engine problems of her aging Chrysler Le Baron. Twice she was also pulled over by police for driving the wrong way on exit or entrance ramps. Her lengthy explanations about impossibly confusing routing managed to distract the police enough that she got no tickets.

The delays meant that she would arrive at her new house a couple days after the moving trucks. To solve that problem she convinced her realtor to let the movers in. She also told him the long list of what furnishings were to be placed in which rooms. Additionally she told him that she expected to arrive exhausted late in the day, and gave him a list of essentials to stock in her refrigerator for which she'd reimburse him later. We were astounded that he supposedly cheerfully agreed to all that. Perhaps it was because she had paid the full asking price for the house with no attempts at lower bids other than the stipulations of the things that required repairs with the amount escrowed until that was done. The realtor also had power of attorney to complete the closing process for her, which he did.

Not finding any of the stipulated repairs done when she arrived at her new home, she called her realtor and her real estate attorney to get that started. She thanked her realtor for having the furniture placed as she'd directed, as well as for having her refrigerator appropriately stocked. More important to her was getting started on the fence so that Princess would have a containment area in the back yard. As Claudia said, Princess was the most valuable relationship in her life, so making appropriate provisions for Princess was unquestionably important.

Slowly, with step-by-step reports and descriptions of the laughable incompetence of the workmen involved, at least the cracked windows were replaced. And, at Claudia's expense, the fence and the gate were completed. She also met in the area a group of women her age. They included her often at their planned luncheons and outings.

Claudia was pretty happy. She explored all the galleries and shops, the recommended restaurants and the town. She made friends with an antique dealer from whom she bought a wonderful French 18ᵗʰ century grandfather's clock as well as a library ladder. She, a music lover, bought season tickets to the Symphony at a Donor level as a method of making connections with potential art buyers. She joined her gated community's Clubhouse that also gave her access to swim as often as she wanted at the community pool. When she was settled in a bit she invited us to visit. Paolo's work schedule wouldn't allow him to go then, so I went alone for a Tuesday-through-Saturday stay.

Her entire house was a wonderful gallery of her artworks, room-by-room featuring her paintings of Monet's garden, magnified flowers, European street scenes, African animals, seascapes, and paintings of Mexican scenes. Her sculptures were excellent accents on surfaces amid her antiques and fashionable lamps and furnishings. It was an exquisite gallery home.

Claudia had a fairly full agenda of things for us to see and do in addition to my volunteering to wheel-barrow the truckload of topsoil she'd had delivered to fill in the boggier areas of her back yard. We visited all the art galleries in town. She warned me to just observe in the galleries and to avoid commentary or conversation. Whenever the owner or manager was in, she'd introduce herself as an artist new in the area. She'd pull out her small albums of photographs of her artworks for them to see. My general observations I later shared with Claudia were that watercolors, usually flower bouquets, palm trees or still-life predominated in the art scene. Her oils and acrylics and their associated much steeper pricing were going to be a hard sell in Charleston.

Those five days with Claudia perhaps were the least conflicted five days I'd ever spent with her. She introduced me in town to any number of women who were becoming her good friends. This included a birthday party potluck luncheon at the home of the ring-leader of a half-dozen of Claudia's peers who lived in Mt. Pleasant. They chose a place to lunch or dine or an activity or place to visit once or twice a month. They called themselves "The Girls." They were sociable, pleasant, long widowed or divorced, with comfortable retirement plans, women who enjoyed the camaraderie of their group.

We toured the wonderful old mansions as part of Historic Charleston Days and she also took me to a Charleston Symphony concert having forewarned me to bring something decently sophisticated to wear. On another afternoon she took me to the Harbour Club she had joined, a place she would eventually convince to exhibit a number of her paintings. I of course reciprocated by taking her to lunches or dinners at places she suggested, as well as a couple cocktail hours at Charleston Place…"another chardonnay, Paolo."

She also agreed to have friends of mine from Hilton Head join us for lunch at her gallery home. Claudia made her excellent Salad Nicoise, and was pleased with my friends' conversation and their admiration of her paintings. She wasn't as happy at Dave's inquiry and interest in her cheetah sculpture. She didn't quote a price, but did say she wasn't willing to part with the original. It was part of what she considered her personal collection. That evening my endurance was tested in listening to her wine-glass-by-wine-glass litany of all the difficulties she'd encountered to reproduce a cheetah for him. Finding a foundry, the trials of patinas, the intricacies of lost-wax procedures were burdensome tasks. The prospect nevertheless reminded her that she ought to get back her boxes of casting moulds from Clarke. She knew, apple of her eye that he was, that he'd take time to drive them down from Raleigh where he was then pursuing his engineering Master's Degree. The time, expense and inconvenience of such a trip didn't occur to Claudia.

Claudia's first year in the Charleston area suited her quite well. She managed once again to find a plastic surgeon willing to take several of her paintings in trade for a facelift. Since the facelift was far more painful and difficult than her California facelifts, "The Girls" needed to tend her and her little Princess for nearly a week of her recovery. Though they fed her, bathed her and tended all her needs, she was unforgiving when one of them broke her favorite teacup.

When she was sufficiently healed she happily attended the Symphony season. She also went to Thursday night bargain buffets at the Harbour Club. She gave us weekly reports of various substantial people she met there, particularly men who she would teach how to dance.

She was pleased that her gated community featured some of her artworks in the Clubhouse exhibit. She also shared an exhibit room with another artist in one of the Charleston mansions as part of a benefit for the Symphony. She spoke of how everybody had loved her artwork despite the fact that they weren't buying. And then she met a gallery operator and his wife who loved her artwork, exhibited it in their Charleston gallery and presented her to other galleries with which they had connections. The man, Chauncy, was a southern Christian who quoted scripture to her on a regular basis. His wife was also an artist. Between them they knew a local printer capable of making giclees. Such print reproductions of her artworks could then be priced to reach a far broader market.

Claudia particularly liked to talk to Paolo about all these business matters. Phone communication with Claudia was steady. She had a system of ringing three times and hanging up. That meant that I was supposed to call her back. Paolo, unbeknownst to Claudia, put a stop to that by answering early. This accomplished his purpose of lowering our phone bill.

Claudia was particularly pleased that Chauncy was going to feature her artwork in a new gallery he was opening in Charleston. There were many delays in that, all of which Claudia found excusable. She bided her time with considering other details relative to the exhibit such as wording and distribution of the announcements, hors d' oeuvres and wine for the reception, and what she'd wear. She also decided that with a French theme and focus on her Monet garden work, she'd sing "La Vie en Rose". So she bought a tape that included Maurice Chevalier singing it in French so that she could relearn the French version. Every few days over the phone she would sing it to me, practicing and testing her recall of the French. Though Claudia's voice as a younger woman was a sensuous cooing that carried a tune, she was totally unaware that voice was gone. When she sang it to me the first time and asked what I thought, I felt so sad about the level of her self-deception that I said, "Well, you better keep practicing."

She did keep practicing, and gave me more telephoned renditions prior to her exhibit reception. These telephone serenades were accompanied by increased confidence on her part, but no melodic or rhythmic improvement. Perhaps she inherited from our mother this need to add one more element of overkill. The difference was that Mother did it naturally and spontaneously. Claudia, on the other hand, was planning and practicing for weeks in advance. As I ought to have expected, the mildest of my suggestions that she forego singing at her reception only solidified her stance that she would sing. Claudia was not seeking assessment or critique in our phone calls, just the self-affirmation that she was practicing. For me, the gag rule, overt or implied, was built into my communications with Claudia, while "no holds barred" was her practice toward me. She was the captain; I was just a deckhand.

Claudia's reception report was that everyone loved the bonus of her "La Vie en Rose." In addition, one of her paintings was sold that night and several others sold thereafter.

Then things about Chauncy started to sour and various suspicions started to surface. There were exceptionally long delays between sales of paintings and receipt of compensation with errors in the calculations. A sculptor who was represented at the gallery reported that he had waited six months and still hadn't been paid for several sales. Claudia was notably disappointed that the young woman Chauncy had hired to tend the gallery was not knowledgeable about art. Claudia expressed her annoyance that the girl hadn't read and committed to memory any of the accompanying information about Claudia. Chauncy and his wife were remiss in returning Claudia's more frequent phone calls and messages. When Chauncy did answer, scripture and prayer were neatly knit into his communications. Gallery and business expansion plans explained the money situation.

Claudia then received a call from her real estate attorney that made her problems with the art world pale rapidly and radically. Week-by-week and month-by-month Claudia's situation went from bad to worse. With sometimes twice a day phone calls from Claudia, it took Paolo and me a while to begin to understand what was going on.

She'd been in the Mt Pleasant house a bit over a year when her real estate attorney called. He was reporting a rumor and speculation to her that proved to be true. The bottom line was that she did not hold a legal Certificate of Occupancy to her house. The builder whose shoddy workmanship had never passed the Village's inspections, eventually, when heads were turned, had forged a signature on the C of O. A discontented secretary in the builder's office had the evidence and eventually decided to blow the whistle on him. Subsequent inspections proved that Claudia's new home not only did not meet code but would require an investment of more than half its value to bring it up to code.

When Paolo and I learned of that estimate we were truly alarmed. We wondered if or when the Village would evict Claudia from her home. Claudia didn't have the funds to make the required improvements, nor should she have been sold a house that was so misrepresented. Fortunately her attorney found her another attorney who would represent her on a contingent-fee basis in a civil suit against the builder. The village at the same time commenced a criminal suit against him for forgery.

Claudia's daily phone calls were soon accompanied either by her sobbing or by her slurring, sometimes both. She understood legal terminology even less than she understood business contracts. In addition, she was suffering vertigo that she asserted was due to the stress of her situation. The vertigo disinclined her from doing much driving. That in turn limited her social life. She had to bypass many a Thursday night buffet at the Harbour Club. She stopped doing activities with "The Girls" unless they could provide total transportation for her.

She also stopped painting. She said she needed to experience moods of happiness or joy in order to paint. Those moods had gotten out of reach. In addition to disheartening circumstances with scripture-quoting Chauncy, and discouraging developments with her lawsuit, her house was in fact starting to fall apart. Not only had no more of the promised repairs been made, but a crack had now opened where the dining room wall met the ceiling. It leaked when it rained, and ants opened it wider when it wasn't raining. A warp in the beautiful wood flooring inside her front door was increasing measurably. The back yard had absorbed the truckloads of dirt we'd added. She thought it was more of a bog that it had been when she moved in. The piers that were supporting her back porch were sinking. She thought the porch was pulling away from the house.

In addition to her lawsuit, the village included her as the associated victim of their criminal action against the builder. Claudia had numerous consultations with attorneys and several depositions and court appearances. She was shocked that the builder and his business-partner wife referred to Claudia as "the rich bitch from California" who was simply greedily after their money. Claudia was dismayed that anyone could entertain the validity of such a description of her. Though Claudia's attorney repeatedly advised her to stay silent and let him do the talking, Claudia couldn't stay silent about the personal insult. She declared "inaccurate" the "money-hungry bitch" label they gave her.

Her civil lawsuit against the builder kept getting bumped and delayed on the civil court calendar. We could barely believe that more than a year of this non-stop misery for Claudia had been going on. We had respites from her sobbing and slurring phone calls only when we traveled out of the country.

When we traveled in the States she had our itinerary and contact numbers that we advised her to use only in case of emergency. We were midway through a California trip when we made our scheduled stop at Asilomar State Park on the Monterrey Peninsula. Having no televisions or telephones in the rustic cabins, and nearly-dark paths in the woods at night, we found three folded notes taped on our cabin door. On the outside of each was written, "Emergency. Please report to front desk immediately." Two phone messages were from Claudia. Their messages went something like "Suicidal. Call immediately" and "Things a mess. Threatening suicide." The third message was from Claudia's former next-door neighbor, Lynette, in Carmel. "Please call."

We'd grown so accustomed to an aura of high drama from Claudia that we were fairly certain that Claudia was okay. Back at the front desk the attendant spotted the notes in my hand, rushed over and said that she also had a suicidal sister, so she knew these messages were not something to take lightly. She said upon Claudia's second call they'd tried to reach Suicide Hotline but weather conditions prevented the call. She considered sending a rescue squad directly to Claudia's as traced by Claudia's phone number.

My first call was to Lynette. Lynette had seen Claudia through some pretty crazy periods, periods when Claudia would roam weeping and sobbing in her own front yard as she'd repeatedly scream at God, "What do you want from me?" Claudia would call and tell me about these episodes. She told me of one time that Lynette walked up, calmed her, soothed her and got Claudia back into her house. Lynette was an even-keeled person.

Lynette recognized me immediately, thanked me for calling, and said Claudia had called her any number of times that day. She knew how dramatic Claudia could be, but in the series of calls Lynette herself wondered if Claudia had gone over the edge of sanity. Lynette wished me well in my call to Claudia.

When I called Claudia and she answered, I held back my fury long enough to learn that nothing catastrophic or exceptional had occurred, and that even though the circumstances didn't make life very much fun for the time being, she wasn't going to kill herself.

Then I gave vent to my fury. My monologue included that she was not to make any such phone calls where she made statements about killing herself, especially to total strangers who believed them. I told her how anxious she'd made the front desk girl who had tried her best to have a Suicide Hotline rescue squad come to her house. I pointed out that if such a rescue squad had provided rumor material for her gated community, surely her court opponents would make a point of her being an unreliable crazy lady, and this would not serve her lawsuit well. I told her that we would call her when we got back to Milwaukee, and that she was not to interrupt our trip again with any non-emergency phone call. Only a life-threatening situation constituted an emergency.

We finished our California trip and picked up the story when got home. The builder and his wife had moved to Florida where they had started a new construction business. They'd taken their yacht and their four-passenger jet with them. Claudia speculated that they'd flee to the Bahamas if either the criminal or civil suits against them made flight look like a better option to them.

Claudia had learned that one of the worst construction foibles of her house was that the chimney's foundation was wood. The roof construction around the chimney was also faulty so that water would trickle down the inside of her master bedroom wall during rains. She was also told that the master bedroom roof was unstable. If the chimney fell on it, the roof was likely to collapse through the master bedroom ceiling, reminiscent of the tree that fell through her bedroom in Carmel.

We agreed with Claudia that no matter what settlement was eventually reached in her lawsuit, she would have to move. We encouraged her to plan moving back to California. She resisted that, but certainly knew she'd had enough of Charleston. With all the unsettled factors and conditions in Mt Pleasant it was impossible to calculate what Claudia would be able to afford or when she would actually be in a position to move. The frustrations accompanying these unknowns added to the sobbing and slurring. Claudia had learned that the builder and his wife had put their six million dollar house in suburban Charleston, as well as their cars, possessions and accounts into a revocable trust for the wife's two minor children. Then they filed for bankruptcy.

Claudia's lawyer discovered that the builder and his wife forged their CPA's signature on their tax returns. Defrauding the bank and the State and Federal government was setting them up for prison terms for far more serious charges than those already on the plate.

While we were still worried about a point at which the village might evict Claudia from her house, Claudia was beginning to understand that even if the Court awarded her a high settlement, the cash might not be available or accessible. The couple had been well advised on how to protect their assets. Their move to Florida, the relocation of their yacht and plane, the establishment of a Trust for her minor children, the filing for bankruptcy were excellent techniques of adding camouflage and setting up an obstacle course.

A break away from the relentless misery would be good for Claudia. Hearing that the Outer Banks held numerous galleries and were the resort and second-home area for East Coast society and nouveau riche prompted Claudia's desire to explore it. Since Daphne's folks had established a couple bookstores there, she wanted their phone number. She'd never met them, but Claudia called Daphne's folks numerous times. She asked for their realtor's contact information. She asked for more highly ranked realtors in the area. She requested that they send her current real estate brochures for the area. Months of research and making connections went into this trip.

Paolo spent several hours daily researching Outer Banks real estate on the computer and mailing hard copy to Claudia of places he thought might suit her. Despite my worries about Claudia's vertigo, and her driving in new territory, Claudia had her maps ready and her routing decided. She arranged for the teenage daughter of a friend to take care of Princess. She arranged to stay several days with Daphne's folks.

In short, Claudia didn't find a house, nor did she find the Outer Banks suitable. Daphne's folks, Fred and Emma, now could count themselves among the Claudia stories. Fred, always a dog lover and current owner of four large dogs, thankfully held his tongue to Claudia's comments that he was feeding, training and treating his dogs all wrong. Fred made himself scarce during Claudia's visit. Emma, the accommodating sweetheart, who maintained a full work schedule at the bookstores, was surprised that on the first night there Claudia asked for Woolite to wash one of her sweaters. Emma offered a number of substitute products for the sweater washing. Having raised two daughters as well as two sons, and having washed many sweaters, Emma could only smile and say, "Oh," when Claudia informed her that Woolite was the only suitable product for washing cashmere sweaters. With a full day scheduled with the realtor the next day, Claudia didn't hesitate to ask Emma to pick up some Woolite for the next evening.

Claudia's report of the trip included both of those stories. She spoke of how commanding and forceful Fred was with his dogs, of how he didn't talk gently with them or give them attention or rewards for good behavior. Claudia also reported that Emma was a wonderful cook who prepared plentiful fine food for her houseguest. But Claudia couldn't believe that a mature woman who dressed nicely wouldn't have a drop of Woolite in the house, and had actually offered shampoo as a substitute. When I protested to Claudia that most people wouldn't expect their short-term houseguests to be washing cashmere sweaters, and that shampoo was frequently used for "delicates" Claudia replied, "Well, at least she has Woolite in the house now!"

Claudia also reported that she'd bought them a nice bottle of wine to have with dinner one night, and she'd given Emma a copy of her self-published book of poetry as a hostess gift.

For the remainder of that year Claudia kept us apprised of the drama, details and developments of her case as her house continued to crack and crumble. Between her being sloshed or sobbing, it was frustrating to decipher the situation, and the prospect that she might well lose everything hung in the balance. During that time Paolo booked us on two ten-day trips abroad to give us some respite.

Nearing year's end we convinced her that she too would benefit from a change of scene, and she agreed to join us for Christmas in Milwaukee. She met Paolo's son, Tony, and his wife and two-year-old son, Alex who joined us for Christmas Day. On other days of the week we visited Milwaukee's art galleries as well as the Calatrava Art Museum that was adding to Milwaukee's fame. We all had a relatively calm and pleasant time during her visit. She was quite subdued while Vicki and Tony were here. If she had any comparative intentions as she repeatedly noted what a darling child Alex was and what excellent manners he had, I let the taps pass.

Still holding the grudge from when he first met her, Paolo, further dismayed by her daily magnum of wine consumption, decided not to pay the price of supplying her with Kendall-Jackson chardonnay. He bought one magnum of it as a starter. Every night when she'd gone to bed he'd use a funnel and fill it with other wine. She made no mention of differences in flavor. Paolo was gleeful about getting away with this trick.

Trials/Trades/Tipsy

During the second year of worries and woes about her house, Claudia went regularly to the library, seeking any light-hearted and amusing books as counter-balance to her misery. She was delighted by the discovery of P. J. Wodehouse. Carl Sandburg's essays and stories also served her well. Another bonus of the library visits was the librarian, a sympathetic listener who also gave Claudia a big hug from time to time. The librarian assured Claudia that her prayer group was praying for Claudia and that everything would be okay.

Claudia was squabbling more with her southern Christian gallery man. Disputes increased about which paintings had or hadn't been sold and what percentage of the sale price went to the artist. The scrapbook of Claudia's personal art history was misplaced by the gallery.

The supply of Wodehouse and Sandburg ceased to keep up with Claudia's demand. My sense of alarm heightened as Claudia's phone messages became indecipherably garbled about elements of the lawsuit. She complained of fatigue, lack of appetite, inability to sleep through the night and preoccupation about the weeds she didn't have the strength to pull that were taking over her yard. Claudia was pleased to hear that I had decided to visit her again.

When I arrived Claudia had chosen a new restaurant along the river for us to have lunch on the way home from the airport. Our first evening went smoothly. I saw the badly warped flooring inside the front door, the water and ant damage in the dining room as well as the crack advancing behind the chimney and through the ceiling of the master bedroom. I also saw the inspector's report that was indeed convincing and alarming. The inspector had agreed to testify as to his findings in Claudia's behalf.

She scheduled our meeting with her attorney for the next day. Despite her myriad complaints about him, her attorney, a satiny-voiced southern gentleman in his mid-forties, had an instinctive sense of strategy, a patient but firm interaction with Claudia and an objective of avoiding a jury trial and achieving a substantial settlement. Claudia had pressed for a jury trial earlier, saying the jury would see her as a poor, struggling artist, good-hearted like them, and that they'd see what liars and cheats had bamboozled her. Paolo and I agreed with the attorney that an out-of-court settlement should be negotiated even though the real estate insurance company was playing a pretty strong game of duck and dodge.

The meeting with the lawyer convinced me of his ability and integrity. We knew he'd been dealing with multiple calls daily from Claudia who'd insisted that his secretary, to whom she'd taken a liking, accompany her as emotional support to the prior hearings. The lawyer accommodated his client as best he could. His secretary chauffeured and attended to Claudia at the hearings in response to Claudia's request. With high stress circumstances, Claudia's vertigo cropped up frequently and raised safety concerns with her driving. All of us knew that on a contingent-fee basis this time-consuming case filled with twists and turns and a formidable cast of characters was too great an investment to lose.

That afternoon, because Claudia had booked us to attend an oyster roast that evening at Dreyton Hall, she needed to take a nap. I started the weeding job, innocent and ambitious. A tireless gardener, I knew that the solution to weeds was to get out the roots. Also I soon learned that rice-bog weeds were far beyond any weed challenges in the Midwest. I would learn soon that the Midwestern garden attire I brought, old shorts and a scoop-necked halter top, wouldn't protect me from other things this turf had in store. Claudia had forewarned me to steer clear of the fire ants, so I did wear garden gloves and borrowed Claudia's rubber clogs. A number of non-mid-western spiders gave me pause as well. That was counterbalanced by my delight of occasionally encountering a small toad or frog. My perspiration seemed to attract the new annoyance of gnats, the smallest barely visible black ones, called No-see-ums in the south, chiggers in the Midwest. I slapped a number of them dead when I saw or felt them bite me.

By the time Claudia got up from her nap I had the wheelbarrow piled high with weeds, and Claudia insisted that I take a long bubble bath in her master bedroom jet tub. Clean and refreshed, on Claudia's advice I wore a long-sleeved T-shirt, jeans, socks, and a pair of her boots to the oyster roast.

The historic plantation home of Dreyton Hall was fun to tour before we headed to the tents on the grounds and started prying roasted oysters out of their shells. I love oysters and had never been to such an event, so the evening was a treat for me. Then my ankles and the back of my beltline started to itch. Despite my being so covered up, the No-see-ums seemed to love my Mid-western flesh. When my tolerance for itching expired, we headed home.

Claudia was in the mood to have more wine when we got home. I joined her, both of us getting looped. She read me a couple funny sections of a Wodehouse book. Then she reviewed our meeting with the attorney. Then she cried. I calmed her. She noticed that I wasn't having another glass of wine with her. She said she knew she drank too much but that life had become such a nightmare. I told her that I'd had too much to drink, that we'd had a productive day, and that we each needed to go to bed. She rambled on about what evil people the developer and his wife were and about how this was supposed to be her dream house. Interspersed with bouts of sobbing, she pondered aloud about everything that had gone wrong with the house, the lawsuit, the gallery representative, former friends and her life. She spoke of how exhausted she was and of how she often didn't even have the energy at night to brush her teeth before falling into bed with her clothes on.

She finally was willing to go to bed but couldn't get herself up from the chaise lounge. I half-carried her to her bed. She was out. I manipulated the clothes off my rag-doll sister, and positioned her in the middle of the bed. This was clearly a night she wasn't going to brush her teeth.

The next morning she moved slowly, customary for her, but made no references and showed no other signs of the previous night's stupor. After breakfast she rambled through East Coast/West Coast comparisons. She spoke of Paolo's being right that she should move back to California. In the Charleston area the food was too rich and made all the women pudgy. She didn't like the Charlestonian mindset that maintained rage-filled pride in the Confederate flag and kept them internally fighting the Civil War. The nearest quality foundry she found for reproductions of her sculpture was in Florida, and even it at great expense put a terrible patina on the horse she'd had reproduced. Such things convinced her that she was a West Coast girl. She wouldn't go back to "the madness" of Carmel. She called Paolo to tell him to look into southern California. She thought somewhere just north of San Diego might work.

Upon completing her call with Paolo, she spoke of whether she and Princess as well as her old Le Baron had the stamina to make it back across the country. It exhausted her to think of crating up her vast collection of paintings and artworks. That statement gave me an opening to say how I loved one of the new large paintings she'd done of Monet's garden that I thought would be perfect in my living room. She asked where I thought I would put it, and I responded "above the fireplace."

She protested, "But you already have my painting there."

I said that I preferred the new one and would trade her.

She said, "But the one you have is one of my finest paintings, and this one is more expensive than that one. Why don't you want the one you have?"

I responded that I thought the colors of the new one were better suited to my house, and that the maroons of the painting I had didn't blend well with my tile floor and my curtains, and unfortunately that I associated the painting with Lou.

She expressed disappointment, if not resentment that I wanted to trade back one of her finest paintings. I told her I was sorry if I'd hurt her feelings and sorry that a trade wasn't suitable. I didn't say and didn't ask the difference in price. I put the idea out of my mind.

Beneath the new painting was a beautiful carved wooden trunk that I nervously opened during the painting conversation. It was full of stacks of hand-written papers.

"What's all this?" I asked.

"It's my poetry," she said as she took out half a dozen of the papers and commenced reading them to me. I think of Claudia as a natural poet. Poetic words and thoughts flow from her, never sing-songy or harshly rhythmic. That led to my suggestion that her ink-line drawings would be delightful accompaniments to a book of her poems. She could pick sixty to a hundred of the myriad poems in that wooden chest, make an ink-line drawing for each and create a delightful book. She liked the idea. It was something she could work on while we awaited the outcome of her lawsuit.

I spent the remainder of the day weeding in her backyard bog, once again in inappropriate garb. The weeds were even tougher in the bog, all too often with roots two feet deep. Claudia had me rush into the house to pour bleach on two nasty fire ant bites. We noticed that I had so many no-see-um bites on my chest and upper back that they looked like a major case of measles. The sight was alarming. As Claudia told stories of how poisonous fire ants are, including that people had died from their bites, my bleach swabbing was followed by applying antibiotic cream that I considered the salve solution to everything. I covered up with clothes as better protection for my next four hours of weeding. As I bathed later, I saw what a target most of my body had been for the biting critters. The fire ant bites on my hand were beginning to fester. The overall itching sensation from the no-see-ums was the worst part to endure, and the massiveness of bites made me contemplate the potential of scarring. I hoped that the itching would subside before I boarded my plane the next day.

Conversation that evening focused on Claudia's decision that she could never in good conscience sell that house to anyone. Even if all the faults were corrected and the house met the building codes of Mt Pleasant, she thought the boggy nature of the property itself couldn't be trusted. She thought the only thing to do was to demolish the house and sell the property simply as a lot. She'd spoken to Paolo about this repeatedly in the weeks before my visit. I was to be the messenger conveying his related proposal. It was that when the lawsuit was resolved and she had moved on to wherever she chose, she should quit-claim deed the property to Paolo. He would oversee returning the house to code and then sell it. From the sale price he would compensate himself to the level of incurred expenses and the remainder of the sale price would go to Claudia. Though Claudia still preferred to have the house bulldozed, and had numerous questions and objections to Paolo's proposal, she did understand that we were willing to assume the burdensome task that she felt no energy or ability to handle. Her sense of relief was visible.

To my surprise she was up and scurrying around the house when I arose the next morning. I was expecting a leisurely morning. She said we had a lot to do. "We need to pack your painting."

My mind raced as I blurted, "Oh, no. I can't afford the difference in price, and it's too big for me to take on the plane."

She responded, "I can't thank you enough for all the work you've done here, and for everything you and Paolo are doing for me. We'll crate it and you can take it on the plane. Then you can pack the one you have in the same crate and ship it back to me. We'll do the trade."

My desire to accomplish the trade was great, but I knew the crated painting wouldn't fit in the trunk of the Le Baron. I again blurted, "Claudia, I love the painting. I'd love to do the trade. That's so generous of you to offer. But the crated painting won't even fit in the trunk of your car."

"Don't be silly, dear heart. We'll put the top down. The crate will fit in the back seat. You're allowed two pieces of check-in luggage, so just tell them it's your second piece," she said.

Reflecting on the weather report for intermittent showers, knowing that my French twist would certainly require reassembly after riding in a convertible to the airport, managing a large crated painting with my luggage through the airport, getting it qualified as luggage, and getting it home when I landed in Milwaukee would no doubt be a hectic and difficult agenda. Troubled that I might squelch the whole deal I nonetheless said, "No, it won't work. Where's your phone book? Let me look into shipping." And after gathering information through a number of phone calls, that's what we did, C.O.D.

In a few days the crated painting arrived at my house. Paolo was also favorably pleased with it as I was. The crate worked fine for shipping back the Lou painting that made its trip east without mishap.

On the art scene in Charleston Claudia learned that her southern-gentleman Chauncy had never paid the printer for the giclees he'd made of Claudia's paintings. Chauncy was also being sued by a couple of galleries in other parts of the country. With that news Claudia drove to the gallery and loaded her artworks from it into her car. A number of paintings were missing, and he still owed her money from prior sales. She enlisted her attorney to represent her in this area as well.

In the New Year the search for a California property for Claudia was on. Progress toward closure on her lawsuit was advancing too. Claudia's attorney managed to get the insurance company re-involved. The Village of Mt Pleasant of course won its criminal action against the builder for his forgery.

Claudia, mourning her loss of rights to swim after she gave up her Clubhouse membership, predetermined that a swimming pool was a necessary feature in whatever California home she selected. We forewarned her of the care and expenses pool-owning friends of ours had reported.

Some magazine conveyed to Claudia that Carlsbad just north of San Diego was considered the ideal place to live. She had multiple phone conversations with Lydia, a realtor for the Carlsbad area. Claudia flew out for a few days of searching. Eventually she chose a forty-five year-old house with about three thousand square feet of interior space in an established neighborhood in the outskirts of Carlsbad. It had no pool but a huge back yard, big enough for her to add one later much as we hoped she wouldn't.

In her lawsuit both sides plus the insurance company had decided to negotiate. Despite all the setbacks and miseries Claudia suffered in the two and a half years of the lawsuit, she proved to be a tough client. She wasn't shy about asking for a large settlement. When negotiations reached an impasse and both sides recessed for reconsiderations, her lawyers suggested to her a reduced amount they thought would be reasonable.

Claudia pulled a nickel out of her purse, put it on the table, and said, "What does this say?"

Her attorneys were nonplussed and eventually answered, "Five cents. It's a nickel."

"No," she said, "Turn it over. See? It says, 'In God We Trust'. That is what you must do. This is the only direction we must take. What we've asked for is already fair, not a penny less."

Back in negotiations the other side proposed nearly a duplicate of the amount Claudia's attorneys had advised. Claudia's attorneys stated that their client was holding firm. Claudia got the settlement she wanted from the insurance company. In addition her lawyer had another construction engineer friend who'd pre-agreed to buy Claudia's property at half-value of her original investment. He'd additionally give her whatever time she needed to close on her new purchase and to pack up and move.

Her call to us with this news was true cause for celebration. We could barely believe the outcome that was far better than anything we'd imagined. Claudia loved telling the nickel story. We heard it many times thereafter.

She called Lydia in Carlsbad to handle closing on the house she'd chosen. It was remarkable that it was still available. I was surprised that the purchase nearly equaled her entire Charleston settlement. Claudia planned to pack and move in sixty days.

We'd already planned a trip to California that now dovetailed with Claudia's arrival in late May. We told her that we could make a few alterations and help her move in. We were surprised, even disappointed, that she declined our assistance. Instead she wanted us to visit for Thanksgiving after she was moved in and familiar with the area. Despite her insistence on that scenario, and despite the risk of her wrath, without telling Claudia, Paolo and I adjusted our trip to surprise Claudia with our visit for a few days just after her arrival.

I was worried about Princess, then age fourteen, being able to survive another trip across country. In fact I'd been progressively worrying about Princess during the course of the lawsuit. Claudia had gotten so fragile, that I thought Princess's death would be the last straw for her.

Nonetheless, Claudia and Princess made the trip from Mt Pleasant to Carlsbad with no reports of mishaps. Her moving truck arrived on schedule and her paintings arrived undamaged. She was pretty well settled in her house when she answered her doorbell to our ring. She was surprised but more importantly glad to see us.

Her two-story house, uniform with the other adobe stucco exteriors in the neighborhood, had a two-story living room and a two-car garage. Sliding glass doors in the dining room and in the family room on the other side of the kitchen led to an expansive U-shaped back yard. The yard had wonderful elevated flowerbeds around the edge and a steep hillside of pretty shrubbery up the back.

Once again she had a jetted tub in the upstairs master bedroom suite. The bedroom next to it had the trundle bed loaded with her collection of Steiff stuffed animals and special dolls. A railing by the stairwell overlooked her cathedral living room. A separate bathroom and the guestroom where we stayed were on the second floor front of the house. Next to it was her library office room. Plentiful storage cabinets and drawers lined the other side of the upstairs hall. Downstairs, off the fireplace-accompanied family room, was the short hallway to the garage. A powder room was on one side of that hall across from folding louvered doors of the laundry area. It was a very nice house.

All the furniture was already in place except for the antique French grandfather clock. It was still crated in the garage. She declined our offer to uncrate it and set it up. She was hiring professionals to do that.

But she was willing for me to break down and bundle all the empty boxes in her garage. And she was delighted that Paolo would rewire the hangers for many of her paintings and hang them in the specific places she had predetermined. With that done we took her to the Coyote Café in town, a place she thought we'd enjoy, where we treated her to dinner. At dinner she told us that she'd called her realtor whom she wanted us to meet and who could join us at an Italian restaurant the next night.

Paolo took care of various minor electrical repairs the next morning. Claudia brought us up to date on scripture-quoting Chauncy. She was still trying to determine how many of her paintings he had that her Charleston attorney hadn't been able to track down. All of the giclees were missing too. Chauncy was an artful dodger. Her attorney had managed to finally stop Chauncy from marketing Claudia's artwork on his multi-artist website. Having her own website was something she definitely wanted to do.

Though Paolo was clear that he had no capacity to establish a website for her, he did know what kind of computer equipment she would need. She would also need high-quality digital photos of the artwork she wanted to post on a website. Paolo was astounded that Claudia who didn't even own a TV, wanted to get the computer and the digital camera right away. They spent through mid-afternoon shopping for and purchasing the computer, printer and camera. While they went shopping, I pruned and weeded.

I was pleased that Claudia got a computer. If Paolo could teach her quickly enough to use e-mail, then I could stop printing and mailing the jokes she so appreciated. I thought it would also provide a better communication system than the stream of phone calls.

We met Lydia the realtor at dinner that evening. She was a soft-spoken, patient, pleasant young woman with a ready smile. Treating Claudia as a friend and not just a client was natural to her. They also shared common interests in plants, flowers and spirituality.

Spirituality was not on Paolo's agenda, and it eluded Claudia the next day when Paolo commenced to teach her the processes and potentials of her computer. She preferred to watch rather than be hands-on. She took copious notes and made numerous lists as Paolo pressed full speed ahead. To me this looked and sounded like a disaster for both of them. An appropriate manual title would have been "Learning Everything about your First Computer and Printer in Less than Eight Hours is

Impossible!" And they hadn't even touched on establishing an e-mail account. Knowing from my own experience that Paolo was masterful at computer work himself, I also knew he wasn't a born teacher. That evening I begged him to put Claudia at the keyboard the next day, and put himself in the side position of coaching rather than demonstrating.

Paolo and I started that day with an early morning forty-five minute walk in the steep hills of the neighborhood. Claudia was up with breakfast ready when we got back. Paolo, who habitually started the day with coffee, wasn't happy that Claudia had no coffee pot. He certainly preferred tea to the packet of instant coffee she found. English muffins she had on hand toasted well in the oven, despite Paolo's sense of that method being a waste of energy. Claudia wanted to master the digital camera so that with Paolo's help they could start photographing the artworks she wanted on her website. It was late in the day before the two of them started the review of computer programs and techniques.

Our air tickets for the next day dictated that we head on home. We agreed however that we'd come back for Thanksgiving.

Paolo's first granddaughter was born in Wisconsin in June, and my first grandson was born in Baltimore in July. Claudia had to take back seat for a while.

It was clear from Claudia's phone calls that she had no recollection of how to send e-mail. She didn't even turn on her computer. She'd lost the copious notes she had taken during her initial computer training. In fact losing, or sometimes finding, a notice or bill on her ledges or in drawers full of accumulated papers, was often a topic of conversation. She'd pontificate about what outrageous articles were in the latest Vogue or Mademoiselle magazine, or she'd be in a state of panic about some financial penalty she'd note on a credit card or bank statement. These penalties were due either to her not having read prior notices or by not having unearthed the bill before its due date. Each phone call held the repeated phrase, "I'm dealing with" usually followed by "madness, foolishness or ridiculousness of P-E-O-P-L-E," a word that she would spell out. Saying the word "people" was obviously too meritorious for fools who didn't deserve to be a whole word. Perhaps spelling the word was also her method of separating herself from those who were so irritating and only worth disdain.

Sometimes Paolo could feed her a method of getting some of her financial penalties reversed. She'd ask him to repeat what he said so that she could write down the exact wording to use.

I was disappointed and annoyed. I had hoped that once the Carolina horror was over, and once she'd gotten back in California, that she'd be her more independent self. Instead it seemed that she'd converted to being needy, that in some way it was generous of her to deliver these endless problems for which we so often had instantaneous solutions. I'd have to wait quite a while before e-mail was part of communication with Claudia.

At Thanksgiving when we flew into San Diego and picked up our rental car, we decided to shop on the way into Carlsbad for a TV for Claudia. We missed access to newspapers and TV whenever we visited her. This shopping sidetrack, however, delayed our arrival at her house by an hour. In that hour she'd called both my sons and our friend Esther who lived in San Diego, alarming them that we hadn't arrived. She'd also called the State Police who assured her that there had been no rental-car fatal accidents in the last hour. I wondered if any reflection of Mother's alarm so many years ago about her being lost at sea had occurred to her in this process.

When we arrived she assaulted us with, "What made you so late? I expected you an hour ago." And when we explained that we'd stopped on the way and bought her a TV she protested that she never watched TV.

Manners were missing on both sides of this fence. We hadn't called to say we'd be late; and she'd said we'd brought a useless gift. Claudia prided herself on being open and honest. For Claudia "open" is sometimes astoundingly and outrageously true, at least in the areas in which she wishes to be "open." But in other areas she's tight as a clam, or as Elli said during that confrontational trip, "You've built a wall around yourself to make it impenetrable to things you don't want to deal with." "Honest" also is a selective process and probably operates in the same modes of self-protection, self-deception, or intentional disconnect as it does with most people.

But, as to manners, Claudia who commented so liberally on my sons' lack of good manners and often on others' lack of them, never seemed to have awareness of polite buffering of honesty. Clanging on her glass at the long ago dinner party to interrupt everyone else's conversation in order to lead the conversation herself wasn't mannerly.

82

Nor was it mannerly for her to tell our guest that if he'd just go home she could go to bed.

The TV was a gift she didn't want and we knew it. We didn't call because she would insist on knowing what we were doing. She'd say no to the TV and have a hissy-fit that we wouldn't hear the end of. We weren't imposing the watching of TV on her. In defense, we thought that on her own she'd discover all the diversity and interest of the Public Television station and perhaps find other shows that would distract her from her sour and sad periods.

Aggravated by Claudia's lack of appreciation, Paolo nonetheless spurted, "We watch TV! We got it for us. We'll watch it when we visit you. You don't have to watch it."

We set up the TV in our guest bedroom. Claudia then asked if it also played videos because she did enjoy videos. So we agreed that we'd take it back and trade it in for a TV/VCR combination the next day. When that happened she insisted that the new one be set up in the family room. That, of course, robbed us of the newscasts since she hated them.

Claudia told us that her realtor, Lydia, would visit at some point while we were there. She also said that the fellow who'd set up her antique clock, who was also scheduled to refinish and repair her Japanese screens, would come for Thanksgiving dinner with his wife and his seven year old daughter. We'd arranged for Esther to come for lunch on Friday to meet Claudia and to see her artworks and her new home.

On Thanksgiving I showed Claudia how I prepared the wild rice dressing and cooked the turkey in a stapled-shut brown paper bag. Paolo and I were both amazed at the amount of wine she consumed before the guests arrived. The fellow and his wife were pleasant company and their daughter was delighted by Claudia's collection of stuffed animals and dolls. They diplomatically overlooked Claudia's slurred conversation.

Thanksgiving went more smoothly than did the next day when Esther arrived mid-morning. Esther had stories and adventures of her own to share, and Claudia clearly didn't enjoy sharing the spotlight. Esther naturally knew more about San Diego than Claudia did. Esther admired Claudia's art but wasn't a potential buyer. And Esther was Claudia's age and among the rare women as well preserved as Claudia. Claudia was happy to see Esther head back home by mid-afternoon.

Computer training during that trip didn't go smoothly either. Though Claudia loved that Paolo could produce various business cards of her paintings for her, she resisted getting on the keyboard. Instead, once again she made copious notes to replace the originals.

Over the next few months before we visited again, Claudia's calls mostly were to Paolo for further computer instruction despite the distance between California and Wisconsin, and despite the differences between their computers. Those calls also conveyed all the difficulties she had in finding someone to set up her artwork website and the complaints of what her website manager perpetually did wrong. But the big item of conversation was that since her neighbors had backed off from allowing her to swim in their pools, she decided to have a pool of her own installed in the back yard. Only one side of her yard held sufficient room between the house and the wall on her property line to accommodate the equipment needed for the project. The equipment and all the ground dug out and all the concrete to be poured had to trek across her front yard. Of course her sprinkling system, front and back, was destroyed, and there were daily worries about her very old poodle Princess being safe with careless workmen, among other things, neglecting to secure the gate.

We knew nothing about swimming pools. Elements of her calls to us about the pool made no sense whatsoever and were particularly frustrating. Occasionally when we would express our frustration she would spend five to ten minutes saying that it wasn't important that we understood what was going on but that it was very important that she could simply vent her own frustrations with us. She after all had been so busy on her house and with her website that she had no time to make friends. Though Lydia was a lovely friend, Lydia's work, unresolved divorce, concerns about her teenage children and other matters left little time for Claudia. And though Claudia liked her neighbor, Darlene, across the street, Darlene and her husband also had full-time jobs. In addition they were still mourning the death of their old dog. And unfortunately they were among the people who told Claudia that they were too uncomfortable about the idea of someone swimming alone in their pool while they weren't home. So they wouldn't permit her to do so. So Claudia felt it wasn't too much to ask us to accommodate her venting. It was something she simply needed us to do.

Over the Edge

W hen we arrived back for her late-February birthday, her new pool was installed, but it was too cold to swim. Not being swimmers, that was fine with us. I missed the large open sweep of her former back yard. I viewed the tall white metal fence around the pool as a harsh disruption of the prior feel. Claudia commented a number of times about how we must be glad that she had such a wonderful place that Clarke would inherit after she was gone and that she had significantly enhanced its value by adding the swimming pool.

She'd made Clarke, the other artist in the family, her sole beneficiary years ago. Despite his retirement from dance to become an engineer, she continued to see him as a sweet-natured spirit like her and the only family member worthy of all the beauty she'd created.

On that trip, one of the seven birthday trips we made to Carlsbad, we bought Claudia a new coffee pot and a toaster. She protested, "But I don't even drink coffee! And I already have a toaster!"

Paolo replied, "Only half of your toaster works and you have to stay with it to manually pop the toast. And the coffee pot is for us. We drink coffee. When we're not here you can store it away."

We'd also brought several packages of specialty coffees we'd been given for Christmas. And we brought several small boxes of chocolates. Claudia had no sweet tooth. Paolo and I were chocoholics. Claudia noticed the decoratively packaged coffee packets on her perpetually cluttered kitchen workspace. She asked about them twice. Both times we told her that they were special coffees we planned to drink while we were there. She also noticed the boxes of candy. About them she said, "Well that's a strange thing to bring. You know I hardly ever eat chocolate."

Paolo retorted, "Well, Claudia, they're not for you. Your sister and I love chocolate. We plan to eat it."

During our stay I was happy to primarily be out of the house while Paolo and Claudia did battle with further computer training.

Claudia's birthday dinner at a French restaurant she'd chosen went very well. So did several other lunches and dinners at places she'd chosen. She was not happy however that we'd arranged to have dinner with Esther in San Diego even though Claudia was of course invited. A former business associate of Paolo's, a woman who'd moved to the San Diego area, was also meeting us at a restaurant Esther had chosen.

Claudia protested that if we were driving all the way into San Diego we should at least dine at a notable restaurant. She'd never heard of the place Esther had chosen. We responded that it was a convenient location for Esther and Carla. The game plan was that Claudia would be with us for cocktails at Esther's first, after which Carla was meeting us at the restaurant. Claudia grew snarly. She didn't like the plan. She didn't see what we thought was so special about Esther. Here we were spending only five days with her and she resented having to spend part of it with Esther and some other person who was a complete stranger to her. I told Claudia that I'd never met Carla before either, so we'd both be having new experiences.

Claudia and Paolo plugged away at computer training during the day of our scheduled dinner with Esther. As I pruned bushes in the front yard, I heard occasional shouting. Paolo would shout, "That's because you don't listen. You've written it down. We've gone over it. You're not listening. You don't listen."

Claudia would shout, "Stop! Stop! I'm brand new at this. That's not what my notes say. I am listening!"

Paolo later told me that of course she would go downstairs to refill her wine glass every time it neared empty.

At lunchtime Claudia gestured to the chocolate and said, "Shall we take some of this as a hostess gift to Esther?"

Paolo stated, "No, we don't need to take a hostess gift. We're treating her to dinner. That will be enough. She doesn't need a hostess gift."

We drove our rental car to San Diego with Claudia in the back. She was the epitome of a back seat driver, exasperating Paolo with noting speed limits, traffic lights, merging traffic and stories from her past driving experiences to San Diego. Paolo held his tongue.

Esther served some light hors d'oeuvres and white wine. As we started into conversation, Claudia reached into her large handbag and pulled out a paper bag of something. She said, "Well, Esther, Paolo and my sister decided you didn't need a hostess gift this evening, but I thought you would enjoy this."

Esther looked in the bag, and said, "What's this?" as she pulled out the contents.

Paolo and I were stunned to see our packages of specialty coffees in Esther's hands as Esther said, "How delightful. You really didn't need to do this" to which Claudia replied, "I thought you would like it."

We were both furious, but exercised a magnificent job of not showing it. Not only had Paolo been clear and adamant about no hostess gift for this occasion, we'd also clearly stated our intentions for the special coffees. Furthermore we knew that Esther didn't drink coffee. She, like Claudia, was a tea drinker. Even if Claudia might later want to be excused for her drunken state, this was a nasty move on her part.

Esther drove us to the restaurant. Carla arrived at the same time we did, so we took care of introductions on the way in. We were seated at a round table for six that left an empty seat between Claudia and Esther. Paolo and Carla conveyed how they'd met and the work they'd previously done together in Milwaukee. Esther shared the story of how we'd met on a European river cruise. She also shared elements of her work, her family, and her life in San Diego. Claudia then drew the small photo album of her artwork out of her purse and told Carla about them.

As dinner progressed, Claudia, increasingly inebriated, would jump into conversations at peculiar points, taking them into one unrelated direction after another. I quietly conveyed that to Claudia. She said she wasn't hearing well and that her placement at the table was a further disadvantage. Then she addressed herself to Carla by saying, "Carla, you have such a beautiful complexion. I hope you won't mind telling me what products you use. My sister does nothing to take care of her skin. She's a fabulous gardener but doesn't even wear a hat or sunscreen when she gardens." I was mortified.

Carla disclosed her products and added that she thought my skin looked very healthy and youthful. Their cosmetic-counter conversation continued with Claudia adding, "I keep trying to get Julia to use some of these things and prevent the awful wrinkles that so much time in the sun creates. Sometimes I get her to wear my garden gloves, but usually she works bare handed."

Esther managed to take the conversation in a different direction and get me off the hot seat.

Before Claudia could jump in again I turned to her and quietly said, "Please don't talk any more about my skin. You embarrassed me."

She looked at Esther, Paolo and Carla who were talking to each other. "Excuse me," Claudia said. Their conversation went on. "Excuse me," Claudia said louder until she got their attention. "Julia just told me that I embarrassed her by talking about her complexion, so I just want Julia and all of you to know that I'm sorry I embarrassed her."

I don't remember who saved the day after that. As the dinner came to a close, I was simply grateful that Claudia had stopped talking and had focused on consuming her dinner and having yet another glass of wine.

On our way home, when Claudia started giving Paolo driving directions, he snapped loudly at her, "I don't want to hear anything more from you. Furthermore, now that you've given away our coffee we'll have to make a stop to buy some so that we have something to drink in the morning. I can't believe you did that!"

Claudia replied, "Well, I'm sorry. You told me we couldn't give her your candy. You don't go to somebody's house for cocktails without taking a hostess gift."

Paolo snapped, "We treated her to dinner. I didn't tell you to give her our coffee."

Claudia went on about how she couldn't understand why we thought Esther was such a special person, how anybody could serve Two-Buck Chuck wine as if it was a special treat, and certainly that we couldn't think there was anything remarkable about the restaurant Esther had chosen.

I was silent. Claudia was so drunk and had so successfully sabotaged the evening that there was no point in conversation. She seemed surprised when we stopped at the store. She'd already forgotten about the coffee.

Back at her house she staggered out of the car and sat down on the sidewalk to search unsuccessfully through her purse for her house key. Paolo had a premonition that she'd ask him to drive back to San Diego for them. He nipped that idea in the bud. "I'm not driving back to San Diego."

Circling the house, I tried the French doors to the dining room, and Paolo tried the ones to the family room. Paolo soon hollered, "Guess what? She never locked this door!" So, we both walked through the house to let Claudia in the front door.

Claudia, up from the sidewalk, hobbled to and through the door and said, "I knew I should have used the restroom before we left the restaurant. I just wet my pants." Wine was doing its job on judgment and bodily function. As sad as this was, Claudia seemed nonchalant, not humiliated or foolish.

When she came back downstairs in her pajamas, she got on the phone. We heard her say, "Esther, dear, will you see if I dropped my keys somewhere in your living room?" After the pause for Esther to search, Claudia went on, "Then I must have dropped them at the restaurant when I got my photos out to show Carla. Would you call the restaurant to find out?"

After Esther called the restaurant and called Claudia to report that her keys were there, Claudia asked Esther if she'd please pick them up and Express UPS them to her. The keys arrived the next afternoon.

Our return to Milwaukee brought another long round of phone calls before we saw Claudia again in late August. We flew into Los Angeles eight days early and visited various favorite California friends on the way to Carlsbad. This time we hadn't given Claudia our air schedule and simply said we'd arrive in the late afternoon. Claudia was miffed that we were only spending five days with her since we'd had additional time that we'd spent with other people. She couldn't comprehend how we could spend time visiting the Californians we'd met on trips when we knew she wanted us to be with her longer. As she put it, "I'm your only sister. How can they be that important?"

Once again my husband worked hard on honing Claudia's limited computer skills while I worked happily in the gardens. Claudia had found new restaurants for us to enjoy with her. She'd also found some good re-sale shops that she knew I loved. We'd stop and shop at them, either coming or going from our restaurant engagements. Every night we'd watch a video Claudia would choose from her collection of favorites: "Some Like It Hot," "Gigi," "American in Paris," "Gentlemen Prefer Blondes." We noticed that she'd fallen asleep during one of them, but we continued to watch it. Suddenly she let out a loud and long blood-curdling scream unlike any I'd ever heard. She slept through it, did it again and continued to sleep.

I turned to Paolo and asked, "What was that?" I expected the neighbors to come dashing over or to be calling the police about some obviously horrendous event that was occurring next door to them.

"Haven't you heard that before?" Paolo inquired. "She does that every night. Usually it's after you've gone to bed. You're such a sound sleeper that obviously you've never heard it."

I was concerned that anyone could sleep through such a gut-wrenching sound. That Claudia herself slept through them was difficult to comprehend. It made me speculate on what night terrors she must regularly experience. No wonder she said that she usually woke up in the middle of the night. The idea of Claudia having night terrors made me sad. It was simply another thing I wouldn't understand. Every visit with Claudia brought some impressive story or experience. This time it was the primal scream.

*   *   *   *   *

We did a lot of worldwide traveling. Claudia always had assignments of what we must see and do wherever we went, but she also resented when we were unreachable. We learned upon our return from a cruise that Princess died while we were away. As Claudia expressed it, "Princess has gone to heaven and I buried her in the back yard." I was surprised at how calm and un-expansive she was about the loss of her best friend. She'd buried Princess in a shoebox far back in her yard with the gravesite marked by a flowering plant. From that event, however, Claudia enlisted Paolo to do massive website research to help her find a new poodle. She wanted one that looked as much like Princess as possible. This proved to be a gargantuan task, and Paolo had to handle the e-mails with the dog breeder. Claudia's e-mail skills didn't meet that demand.

Claudia had very limited typing skills too. Though occasionally she forced herself to use her antique typewriter to copy a business letter, handwriting was otherwise her method for all her poetry and everything else. She refused my offer of my old electric typewriter, saying that electric typewriters always repeated letters because she couldn't lift her fingers quickly enough. Claudia had written a lengthy play about her Mt. Pleasant house experience, a play she felt certain Hollywood could use. She'd written it in longhand. I volunteered to type it for her. Typing a play that was loaded with underlining and exclamation points was indeed a challenging experience. She submitted it to the daughter of a friend who had Hollywood connections. To my knowledge nothing ever came of it.

Yes, phone calls continued. She was disappointed that we were going to visit Clarke's family in Annapolis for Thanksgiving. And though we invited her for Christmas, she declined it as a trip she couldn't afford.

Valentine's Day was the day Claudia considered most significant. She seemed to measure her significance in people's lives by whether they sent her a Valentine and whether the card was particularly beautiful or laughably funny. She called on Valentine's Day this year to thank us for our card, but mainly to say she was very disappointed in Clarke. "You know what he sent me...an old Christmas card!"

I laughed. I said it was probably because Clarke was swamped with work and with responsibilities that he didn't have time to shop for a card. Furthermore, he'd known me to send whatever card I had on hand. At various times after he'd left home I'd probably sent him a Christmas card for his birthday. He no doubt thought she'd understand and be amused.

She wasn't amused. She'd called him and told him so, as well as everything else she'd said to me earlier in her call. She said, "Clarke knows how important Valentine's Day is to me. I ask very little from him. Four cards a year is all I ask: a Valentine's card, my birthday, Christmas, and any one of the other holidays or a note to tell me what's going on in his life. He knows he'll inherit my estate when I'm gone, so just four cards a year isn't too much to ask."

Her call to him angered her further. Though he apologized, he offered no explanation and was basically silent. Since her birthday was ten days after Valentine's Day, she certainly hoped he'd redeem himself.

When she launched into my failure of conveying social graces to my sons, I told her she'd always been critical and abusive to me about my parenting skills. I told her that despite my own faults and inadequacies I was proud of my sons and their personalities and accomplishments. I told her that her system of setting up four obligatory cards a year was no way to build a relationship and certainly no way to be assured of love.

Later Claudia called to say that Clarke had sent her birthday card. It was black and not funny. She'd left messages on his answering machine but hadn't gotten through to talk to him. She was hurt and angry. She'd called Clarke's father-in-law and left a message on that machine saying that Clarke was behaving badly and that his daughter and grandchildren were at risk of losing the inheritance of her entire estate.

Paolo was on the extension phone as he usually was when her calls came in. I was so furious that it was good that Paolo did most of the talking. Since she hadn't heard back from Clarke or his father-in-law, she had contacted her attorney to proceed with the associated changes to her Will and Trust. She closed her conversation with, "Tell them I wish them well, but I haven't worked my whole life to leave my estate to someone who won't even send me four cards a year and show me some love."

We, of course, were also involved in a series of empathetic and apologetic calls with Clarke and Daphne and her folks. Claudia had outdone herself with this episode. My fury about it was enormous but useless. Claudia, the spirit of joy and beauty, would never understand or take ownership of the damage and destruction she created.

I thought of the excellent book I'd read, <u>I Hate You, Don't Leave Me,</u> about personality disorders. I recalled from it how alcoholism often is a screen for deeper problems. Rather than my formerly opting for the fuzziness of the "borderline personality disorder," the more identifiable aspects of "bi-polar" fit Claudia. She'd earned the label "alcoholic" decades ago. On occasion, when she scared herself, she'd substitute grape juice for wine for a few days. But she would never stop drinking. The payoffs of her wine-assisted masterful manipulations offered no motivation for her to stop or to abandon those ploys.

I remembered Claudia's appearance in that long-ago family photo. Mother's Christian Science background contributed to her not recognizing the early signs of Claudia's problems. I speculated on alcoholism in our family line via Dad. I speculated on the previous generation's prevailing shame about psychological problems. Since Claudia's childhood, the advances of psychology, psychiatry, therapy and medications have helped those with bi-polar disorder function in a more balanced way. Who would Claudia have been had she been treated?

She certainly had been a source of much hurt, abuse, anger, and frustration in my life. The litany of episodes was so easily on tap. I wanted to spit them at her, to rant and rail with my anger. Did all the others who'd abandoned her or been abandoned by her feel contentment and peace? Was there any value in confronting Claudia whose resistance to owning-up to such assertions was so well ensconced? My answer was no.

We took our California trip and stayed at Claudia's for a few days over her birthday. She showed us the black card and said, "Do you think this is funny?"

It actually was a funny card, but I simply said, "I'm not going to talk about it." I was on-guard to avoid discussion of her harangue with Clarke. I also recalled my out-of-body experience long ago when I'd confronted her about marketing her artwork. I knew I was on the edge of becoming that out of control.

She showed us copies of her changed Trust indicating that Paolo and I were the inheritors of her estate. From time to time she would say, "When I go to Heaven you'll have all this."

Paolo would respond with things like, "Ah, Claudia, you'll probably outlive all of us."

I'd say things like, "You never know. You know in our family, deaths weren't chronological. Remember, Aunt Margaret lived to one hundred four. You might have thirty years left. Who knows what all might change by then."

Claudia had hoped that she'd have her new puppy by her birthday, but the breeder told her not to expect to receive her little white poodle for another month. In the meanwhile, progress and changes on her website held her attention. She got excited about the prospects of various buyers who proved to be scam artists. Fortunately she didn't lose any of her artworks to them.

*   *   *   *   *

We visited for a few days again in September, combining a stop in Carlsbad with our plans to see my former stepdaughter who was a contestant in the Mrs. America contest in Palm Springs. At Claudia's we were introduced to her tiny new dog, Celeste. Though Celeste had a dog door through the garage onto a contained area outside, she still wasn't house broken. To keep Celeste contained, the wood-slatted doors were set on their sides again, to block the passage between the kitchen and family room, and from the family room into the front hall. Getting over them required action like getting on a man's bicycle. During the course of a day we crawled over these horizontally placed doors numerous times. We asked Claudia why she hadn't gotten a folding screen to solve this problem. She didn't like the idea of attaching it to the wall. She also said they were expensive.

Our computer work, gardening and dining out went as usual. So did Claudia's wine consumption. By late afternoon she was slurring and staggering. One afternoon when I was inside reading I heard a crash and broken glass. I ran to help her up where she'd fallen on the other side of the slatted barricade in the family room. She'd brought in the wine glasses from the table on the patio. She had bloody scrapes on her arm and leg but was still holding onto the broken glass.

"I'm okay. I'm okay," she repeated as I helped her up and ran to get a cold washcloth. She refused to have any antibiotic ointment or bandages put on her scrapes.

Later that same evening after we'd come home from dinner I heard a noise in the dog run outside the family room. Claudia came through the garage hallway into the room with more bloody abrasions on her legs.

"What happened?" I blurted.

"Oh, nothing, I just let Celeste in."

"But you're bleeding."

"Oh, I must've bumped into something. It'll be okay."

The falls frightened me. Paolo shopped the next day and found an expandable screen for the space between the kitchen and the family room. Its installation was a great improvement over crawling over the old doors.

The next day Claudia invited her neighbors Darlene and Carl over for wine and cheese at seven o'clock, after Darlene's long commute home from work. Darlene had asked what she could bring, and Claudia had told her we were sweet-tooth people. Darlene was bringing special homemade cookies. To me the combination of the time and the cookies meant that Darlene and Carl were under the mistaken assumption that the evening would include dinner.

Claudia, Paolo and I had a late lunch that afternoon, knowing that cheese, crackers and wine would have to satisfy any further hunger we might have that day. Claudia popped open the first bottle of champagne as Darlene and Carl arrived promptly at seven. Darlene opened a large box of cookies she'd brought, telling us that if Claudia was right in her sweet-tooth reference to us, she knew we'd enjoy these. She looked a bit surprised that we each took and ate one immediately. We raved about their excellence.

Claudia had already placed the cheese-and-cracker tray on the coffee table in the living room where we all sat. Claudia spoke about the computer training Paolo was helping her understand. Since Carl hadn't been in her house before, she told him about various artwork and furnishings in her living room.

Later, as Claudia went to the kitchen to bring in another bottle of champagne, Paolo and I asked Darlene and Carl to tell us more about their backgrounds and their jobs. Darlene spoke first and not at length when Claudia came back and poured another round. Claudia accompanied that with talk about her website and the difficulties she had with her website designer.

Paolo told Claudia that we'd asked Carl to tell us more about themselves. With Paolo's encouragement, Carl spoke well and enthusiastically about the medical research being done at the lab where he worked. Paolo and I found it fascinating and interjected occasional questions. Claudia struck up a side conversation with Darlene.

Carl's work involved the equipment and systems to keep oxygen and circulation effective during open-heart surgery. He did a good job of explaining the whys and wherefores and the advances being made particularly to avoid stroke during surgery. Time was passing. The cheese and crackers were disappearing. Once again it occurred to me that they probably thought the gathering was for cocktails and dinner, though no actions or aromas were indicating dinner.

Claudia directed her gaze at Carl and said, "I think we've heard enough about what you do, Carl."

Paolo and I both protested that our conversation with Carl was midstream and we wanted to learn more. Carl immediately apologized to Claudia saying that he loved his work and that it wasn't the first time he'd gone on too long about it. I asked him to finish the part that had been interrupted.

Claudia got up, took Paolo's hand and said she needed his help to open another champagne bottle in the kitchen. I asked Carl to wait until Paolo was back because he'd like to hear the rest too. In the interim I asked them if their backyard pool had to have a separate fence around it. I'd been surprised by the fence at Claudia's since her backyard area had a high fence. They said there wasn't a separate fence around their pool, and that I should come see it at some point. They speculated that regulations must have changed since their pool was installed. I was still talking with them about that when Claudia and Paolo came back with the third or possibly the fourth bottle of champagne.

Claudia immediately said, "No more of this unpleasant talk about surgery."

Paolo said, "You interrupted Carl. I want to hear what he knows."

Claudia smugly said, "No, no more."

She'd barely gotten that out of her mouth when Paolo shouted loudly at her, "Damn it! You don't always have to be the center of attention. You think that you and your artwork and your self are the only things of interest in the world. You don't always have to be the damned center of attention. I want to hear what Carl has to say. So sit down and be quiet."

I was aghast. Paolo never behaved like this. He was over the edge, out of control, and I automatically blurted breathily, "Paolo!" in hopes of restoring his sense of social awareness.

"I'm sorry," he said adamantly, "but why does she have to be so selfish and self-centered? I'm tired of it."

Claudia beckoned to Darlene. "There's something I want to show you in the family room." Darlene went with her.

Paolo said to Carl and me, "I'm sorry for my outburst. Sometimes she just irritates the hell out of me."

Carl apologized again and added that he'd probably had too much champagne after a long day and that it was time for him to go home.

I asked if I could go with him and just take a glance of their backyard and pool, to which he agreed. As we left, Carl said to tell Darlene to come home whenever she was ready.

When I returned, Paolo had gone upstairs to the computer room. I took the empty cheese tray to the kitchen and cleaned it. Claudia was showing Darlene more artwork in the family room. I thanked Darlene once again for bringing the delicious cookies. I told her that Carl had given me a quick tour of their back yard, and how beautifully I thought they'd landscaped it. I told her that my large dose of fresh air while gardening had caught up with me and that I needed to be excused to head off to bed.

The next morning Claudia once again showed no sign of a hangover even though she'd consumed nearly her customary magnum of wine before the champagne. Her only references to the night before were that she thought her neighbors had enjoyed getting to know us, and we had the benefit of Darlene's cookies that we were clearly enjoying.

Back in Milwaukee, I couldn't get Claudia's injurious falls out of my mind. For the next several months I worried about whether an incoming call might be from neighbors or paramedics having found Claudia bleeding in her home. Fortunately no such calls came. Phone calls from Claudia continued, however. She was now using email. She was particularly excited about one she'd received from a person in Africa saying she would receive nearly a million dollars for allowing a politically displaced family to use her bank account to route their vast fortune out of their now insurgent-controlled country. Claudia wasn't happy to hear from Paolo that it was a scam. She was equally unhappy that notice of her winning the United Kingdom lottery was also a scam. And when she complained of having too many expenses, especially since she was still paying for having the exterior of her house painted, Paolo reminded her of several ways he'd previously told her to save money. Her phone service was expensive and didn't begin to compete with phone plans that would save her a lot of money. Her security system cost more than four hundred dollar a year, a system she had installed in order to get a discount on her Homeowner's policy. She never learned how to operate it, so it was truly of no value to her security. He finally got her to avoid a fifty dollar monthly fee for the credit card processing she'd arranged with her bank to handle purchases from her website. She had made no website sales.

Claudia was also concerned about art magazine articles she read about thievery from art websites. Thieves would copy artwork and sell them as originals. She spent more money to have all her artworks copyrighted, and more again to have a computer assistant she hired to do a special process on the photos of painting on her website so that they couldn't be easily copied. She'd also seen an "Art and Antiques" magazine that promoted artists and their websites, so she paid seven hundred fifty to be included in an issue.

For decades she thought she'd win the Reader's Digest Sweepstakes. Keeping in the running for it explained the numerous magazines she stacked up everywhere. She continued to get Vogue and Mademoiselle because of her history with them, but she thought most of the fashions in them were an abomination. She was regularly distressed with articles about the hottest new artists and the huge prices paid for their works that she found ugly, violent or perverse.

Claudia expected that someday a wonderful rich man would discover her artworks and become a collector and patron. He would also find such a remarkable, talented and fascinating spirit as she, irresistible. "Happily ever after" would eventually arrive.

The "I'm dealing with" phrase continued. I finally asked her to stop using it, explaining that it sounded as if things were burdensome, tedious coping problems. I told her it didn't make her sound joyous. I felt burdened and unhappy just to hear it.

I should have known better than to mention it. She explained that "dealing with" meant that she was handling or taking care of these things, not that she was burdened or unhappy. The phrase persisted even more often thereafter.

Birthdays/Buddhas/Aging

Paolo decided that we should join Claudia for her seventy-fifth birthday. We choreographed another February trip including visits with our California friends.

Claudia chose a flamenco restaurant in San Diego for her birthday dinner. Paolo told her in advance that he no longer liked to do distance driving at night. Claudia invited Lydia to be our guest in exchange for her doing the driving. At the restaurant a superb classical guitarist and three highly skilled female flamenco dancers provided the accompanying show to an excellent meal. Special desserts with sparklers in them were provided to guests celebrating birthdays. The celebrants were also invited to improvise dance along with the flamenco dancers. Claudia did that with a big smile and wide-open eyes the entire dance. She also took the microphone and told everyone that as a gift to them she was going to sing a Spanish song, which she did. It was a fun evening.

This particular visit was not tainted with any notable blowups, mishaps or embarrassments. It was our only Carlsbad trip that year. Other people, places and things dominated our time before we returned for Claudia's seventy-sixth birthday. Our trip had been delayed by a month or more because of other trips we'd booked. In that interim Claudia had become more solicitous about what was going on in our lives, and she was complimentary about our projects and involvements with our local community. Those inquiries and particularly the compliments were pleasant and surprising changes in her interaction with me. Her prior predictable comments, "I don't know what you find interesting in those people" or "I don't know why you waste your time on such nonsense" disappeared.

Claudia, having explored and abandoned a senior-citizen group, the Red Hat group, and a Newcomer's group, managed to "deal with" the trials and tribulations of a group of older women artists. That at least provided artwork exposure in new locations for Claudia. She found most of the members neither interesting nor talented but enjoyed the company of a couple of them. She locked horns with others who protested Claudia's ways of doing things.

She regularly reported problems with Celeste. The dog had weepy eyes that left red marks on her face fur. No expensive prescriptions or dog foods provided solutions. Nor was there any solution for the naturally snarled coat Celeste inherited in her breeding. Bathing and brushing Celeste and the sharp-toothed nips that accompanied them eventually prompted Claudia to try various professional groomers. The results never measured up to their expense. Nonetheless, Claudia found that Celeste was better behaved when Claudia spoke to her in French, so progress in that way was made in Celeste becoming a more manageable dog.

Claudia's swimming pool continued to be a problem. She had major branches taken off a large tree near the pool to help solve filtration problems. Perhaps in observing the tree work, her neighbors then protested the threat to their property of Claudia's large old front yard tree with its branches hanging over their yard. Removing its overhanging branches proved not to be enough. In time she had the entire tree removed and that required the removal of her front bushes and plants as well. Everything was an expense.

But more alarming to Claudia than the pool or Celeste's eyes and coat, was word on the street that coyotes had been spotted in Carlsbad. Claudia accumulated a cluster of coyote reports that included a sighting right on her block. Such a presence was an unacceptable threat to people who had pets, particularly people who had expensive delicious-looking little white poodles that stood no chance against a coyote. Claudia tried to involve village government, the S.P.C.A., San Diego County, and her neighbors in this coyote concern; however, the most productive step that was taken was her own. She paid Miguel to remove the majority of brush from her backyard hillside. This at least prevented coyotes from having protective cover while they lay in wait for an unattended Celeste. Unfortunately Claudia's door-to-door campaign to enlist her neighbors to also remove unnecessary brush from their yards only contributed to her neighbors' sense of annoyance.

We took no TV's, toasters, coffee pots or anything of note on our belated birthday visit. We arrived the day before Claudia's scheduled lunch at home with San Diego Museum's curator of Asian works. The curator was to see the collection of rubbings from Angkor Wat and other Cambodian shrines that Claudia was willing to contribute to the museum.

As we awaited the curator's arrival the next day, we were surprised by Claudia's calm as three messages arrived from the curator explaining one delay after another. Claudia's ratatouille was postponed and postponed. Claudia's wine consumption was not. We shouldn't have been surprised by this, but we were.

During the delay, Claudia informed Paolo about the details of the Buddha collection she had on her family room mantel. One by one she told the story of how she'd attained each Buddha, the century from which it came, and the negotiated price at the time she bought it. I, having heard this dissertation a decade ago, and again possibly another decade before that, realized that I didn't absorb and retain such information. With the opportunity at hand, I grabbed a notebook and pen and asked Claudia to talk us through the Buddhas once again.

She was annoyed and demanded to know why. My explanation prompted her to say, "Oh, so you think I'm going to die soon." That response surprised us. She nonetheless told the stories of the Buddhas again while I took notes as rapidly as I could.

The belated but totally charming and highly qualified curator finally arrived. Lunch conversation, exchange of information and arrangements for the future went very well. It was a thoroughly enjoyable afternoon. Claudia would do the follow-up after our visit.

The next day we took a scenic drive through horse country to the pretty town of Falbrook. Its community art gallery held the exhibit of selected items of an annual art competition. From the excellent variety of paintings, sculpture, and pottery each of us chose entirely different artworks that we thought might win the show's top prize. We also ate wonderful lunches at the gallery's connected restaurant. Then we visited the fascinating gems and stones exhibit at the casual museum across the street. It was there that we got the phone call from Zak and Chloe in New York announcing their plans to be married in Paris at Thanksgiving. Claudia was of course especially pleased that Zak would be marrying a girl of French lineage.

This visit with Claudia was going quite pleasantly until bedtime the next night. Paolo was upstairs dabbling on the computer when Claudia and I finished watching a Peter Sellers video. After I'd gotten into bed, I heard Claudia calling to Paolo. She needed his help right away with the video machine. As it turned out she'd encountered a glitch in rewinding the video. She'd also noticed that the folding gate we'd gotten to keep Celeste contained had pulled loose from the wall. These two problems coupled with Paolo's observation of Claudia's inebriated incompetence, and her "right now" demand for him to attend to them, made him snap with fury reminiscent of the time Paolo lost his cool when Carl and Darlene visited. I decided to stay in bed and out of the fray.

Paolo solved the video and the dog gate problems. He was still seething as he entered our bedroom and spewed out, "I told her we're leaving tomorrow. We're not staying here anymore."

In a whisper I reminded Paolo of a couple of engagements and meetings with people that were still on our agenda at Claudia's. Departures from them would be harshly embarrassing.

We also listened to Claudia making phone calls to the long-term and long-distance friends she'd maintained. When Claudia got very drunk and was very distressed, they too were on her call list. This time she was telling the others how distressed she was that her brother-in-law had just blown up at her. She described how he knew how technologically inept she was, and how he'd never objected to fixing her VCR before. After a pause she said, "Well, they did have a couple martinis before dinner."

Balancing all the elements at play the next morning, when Paolo came down to breakfast he immediately said, "Claudia, I don't want to discuss it, but I do apologize for shouting at you last night. I apologize. Enough said."

She accepted the apology, and no more was said about the incident. The remaining agenda and gatherings occurred for the next day and a half. It wasn't until we stopped for a pre-arranged visit with our friends in Corona del Mar that we realized that we had in fact left Claudia's a day early. Claudia made no mention of it either. Fortunately our friends were at home and flexible. Paolo was still angry at Claudia's sense of entitlement to be so instantly demanding. He continued saying that he had no interest in visiting Claudia ever again.

Paolo had been the most helpful and longest-term ally Claudia had ever had. In the previous year she'd already established a phone pattern that focused on Paolo. If he answered the phone she didn't even ask to speak to me. And Paolo knew he too needed to make no effort to include me in the calls. Though I'd become more assertive in letting Claudia know how she treated me as a "no count" person in a perpetual "no-win" situation she did soften her treatment of me in the upcoming year. She was clearly more invested in letting both of us know how helpful we were to her and how she appreciated our assistance with ways for her to cope with or resolve difficulties she encountered on a daily basis.

She also decided that she was in fact getting old. She felt reductions in her energy. She was tired far more often. From time to time she thought she was going to die. My taking down the information about the Buddhas had provoked her into these thoughts of death. Her mission became a matter of organizing and planning to ship to us all the papers we'd need for her wishes to be carried out when she "went to Heaven." She planned to send us her house key, her Will and Trust, and other papers and references we'd need.

As time passed, her phone calls indicated all the death arrangements she was making and all the details that we needed to know. Most of these conversations were with Paolo, sometimes on speakerphone so that I could be informed as well. Usually when she spoke with me she wanted to read me new poetry she'd written about the journey she was on, and about advice to others on how to think positively. The content and messages of these poems had remained consistent for decades. From what I considered my logical and reasonable point of view, the tragedy was that somehow she couldn't help herself with her thesis of joy and beauty, her meditation, her knowledge of foods and diet, her endless lotions and her facelifts. Many elements of her life were like her dogs that could dance and do tricks and even understand French, but never got house broken.

Apparently because she was still making periodic payments to her attorney and accountant for the money she owed them, it took several months for her to receive copies of her updated Will and Trust. When she got the copies she realized that her realtor Lydia was listed incorrectly on them, so Claudia had to pay for the papers to be reworked. Claudia's conversations about such things were never clear and concise. I couldn't tell if Lydia had been listed as the primary beneficiary or whether she'd simply been listed as the first person to contact if Claudia were found dead.

More months went by without the arrival of the papers and the key. During that time Claudia inquired more actively about the work we did for the theatre and neighborhood organizations we belonged to. She was mystified that we voluntarily did these things and that we stepped in to fill a need to help our community. She became downright laudable about it.

With the presidential campaign ongoing, one day Claudia called and said that Hillary Clinton was really off her rocker with her health plan. This was astounding since Claudia never talked politics. Claudia nonetheless conveyed that she thought Hillary's expectations that people could privately fund all sorts of medical treatments were outrageous. Paolo encouraged her to write a letter to Hillary.

Within a few days, Claudia called Paolo to ask for Hillary's address and to read him the letter she had written. The letter told Hillary that Claudia's social security and pension provided about fifteen hundred monthly which barely covered Claudia's basic needs. It told Hillary that Claudia, as a successful artist whose painting of a seascape was in the San Francisco Federal Building, still had to pinch pennies at every turn and deny herself small pleasures and opportunities on a daily basis. Claudia advised Hillary that many people simply couldn't afford health insurance and that Hillary's expectations were outrageous.

By the next week Claudia wanted to know if we'd seen Al Gore's movie and what we thought of it. Within a few days she'd composed a letter to Gore offering to help save the environment. She told him of her lifetime as a struggling artist, of her age now giving her some limitations, of her seascape in the Federal Building, of her powers to inform and convince people, of her memberships in two Carlsbad organizations and what she planned to present to them to further Gore's mission to save and balance the natural world.

Far more worrisome, Claudia reported taking a pretty nasty fall down the stairs. She was badly bruised and quite scared by it. She didn't say what time of day or conditions that prevailed at the time of her fall. I was afraid to ask. She reported that her chest hit the Newell post that broke her fall and kept her from slamming into the wall at the landing. Her chest was so badly bruised that she couldn't put on a bra. She had bad bruises up and down her arm and a large lump near her shoulder, but she was sure nothing was broken. She hadn't gone to the hospital. She was quite argumentative about that. Why would she go to the hospital for things Medicare wouldn't cover and for unnecessary tests since she already knew she was okay? I told her it sounded as if she might have dislocated her shoulder.

On her call to us the next day, she said she thought I'd been right about the dislocated shoulder. She had manipulated it a lot that morning and she thought she'd popped it back into place.

Ten days later she said that she'd awakened in a high state of agitation in the middle of the night. That comment was one I'd heard repeatedly over the years, though she picked and chose about whether she regularly was a sound sleeper or a regular distressed awakener. In any case this time her shoulder awakened her. She described how she went to the bathroom and watched in the mirror as she massaged and manipulated her shoulder for about twenty minutes. Then she suddenly felt sick to her stomach and had to race to the toilet to vomit. She said she vomited a lot and that the vomit had a lot of strange yellow stuff in it for which she had no explanation. She felt that her shoulder was fine now.

She wanted to know when we were going to come visit her. I told her that our travel agenda was full until mid-January and that I hadn't even memorized the itinerary of the cruise we were taking the following week. She mentioned that she'd earned airline miles that she might contribute for one of our tickets, but she didn't pursue the matter.

She called Paolo the next day asking him if we'd come again for her birthday in February. Paolo said he'd left that decision in my hands and that he knew I was swamped in finishing a number of other things before we left on our cruise. I told her we'd join her for her birthday.

The week before our cruise commenced was the week of severe California fires. Our first news of it was from Claudia who said her neighborhood hadn't been asked to evacuate yet, but she was getting ready. In three sequential calls to Paolo she was telling him what she was packing into her car, and he was advising her of other things she needed to take along including her homeowner's insurance policy. Despite the drama she was creating, she was also impressively calm and level headed. She even gave us the phone numbers of her local fire and police departments as well as the announced probable shelter Carlsbad people would use if the flames came nearer.

Before we flew to Rome for our cruise, the Santa Ana winds had died back. The California fires seemed to be under control, and we felt

Claudia and her home would survive the interim. That she did, without having to evacuate her property.

Our next birthday trip started with a few days of staying with and visiting friends in San Diego before we drove on to Carlsbad. Lydia, her friend and ours, came over for supper and brought several varieties of excellent cookies from her new business.

After dinner the noise I thought was frogs came up strongly. It was as if the Holy Roller Choir of Frogs was singing at full gusto under Claudia's bedroom window. As soon as I turned the patio light on and stepped outside, they fell silent. Not five minutes after I'd gone back inside and turned the light off, the sound reached its next crescendo. On my next flashlight trip I found the frogs hiding under the lip of the lily pond. This was a treat for me, but I wondered how Claudia could sleep with the volume they created. Perhaps it was one of the benefits she had with her increasing difficulties hearing. Claudia drank to excess as usual, but thankfully it didn't result in any conflicts or incidents.

While in her stupor that evening Claudia reminisced about her sail from Bahamas to Florida those years ago when Mother thought she was lost at sea. Rather than "fun and fine with friends" as she'd reported to Mom, Claudia disclosed that the sail was with two attorneys she'd met on the Bahamas. The attorneys were so blitzed and stupid, that Claudia chose to swim next to the sailboat most of the time. They got stuck on a sandbar, cured only by a long wait for the tide; and the lawyers proved of no value to the Bahama property idea. Claudia knew that "open and honest" wasn't a good idea for her report to Mom, or to her husband at that time, but she made no apologies for the incident.

The next day we enjoyed the treat of going to Carlsbad's Musical Instrument Museum to see a variety of classical and pop instruments. Sometimes by pushing a button, short videos could be played. Frequently a whole series of musical highlights or examples through the decades was accessible by pushing buttons. Seeing us bounce or sway or lip-sync as we pushed buttons, Claudia pushed some buttons too. That caused her to realize that she wasn't hearing the things that were making us dance and smile. When she told us, we realized how impaired her hearing was.

Next, at La Costa grounds and spa where we lunched, Claudia, a devoted fan of Depak Chopra, said she couldn't understand why nearly all of its sales clerks were fat and unattractive, conditions that weren't exemplary of the philosophy, techniques and products marketed there.

For her birthday, Claudia had booked brunch in La Jolla at the famous Valencia Hotel, a preferred place for the rich and famous since the 1920s. It was a windy day with the threat of showers, so we brunched in the main dining room. The wait-staff kept filling our champagne glasses until we learned through observation that you had to clearly decline to get them to stop. Paolo was stunned that Claudia would signal for more champagne when her glass was still more than half full. I had noted long ago that Claudia always topped off her glass well before it was empty. I attributed that habit to her not wanting to log the number of glasses she'd had. Each year I saw the drinking more in charge of her than her being in charge of it. She said she drank too much because of stress. To me her level of alcoholism had a life of its own, teasing her into finding nearly anything sufficiently stressful so that it could have its way with her.

Nonetheless we had a wonderful brunch and went on to a number of galleries. Claudia, with a town map in hand, thought she knew where she was going, but we'd walk several blocks and she'd say, "Well, it should be right here." But it wasn't. So we just followed her into whatever gallery she picked. One of her old sandals fell apart. She took them off, left them on a street bench, and went into the next two galleries barefoot.

On the way home, she said she'd had a terrible experience in the last gallery because she wasn't able to hear what the clerk was saying to her. Between that and not being able to hear at the Music Museum the day before, she knew her hearing was sufficiently impaired and she'd simply have to get hearing aids in order to be able to continue doing business, marketing her artworks.

The next day was weeding day for me while Claudia and Paolo looked on the computer for hearing aid information. Claudia was upset that hearing aid expense that could run thousands of dollars, but she was now convinced that the hearing problem had to be solved.

That evening Claudia's friends, Lydia and Gina came for dinner. Gina was the person who'd agreed to adopt Celeste if Claudia died. Lydia brought Claudia a pretty plant for her garden. Gina arrived with a prettily wrapped bottle of wine and a special artwork, silver-plated wine cork.

Claudia had been sipping and topping off her glass of wine since nine in the morning. Every visit we noted her earlier start-time. Claudia was already slurring when her guests arrived. The hearing-aid research had done nothing to lift her spirits.

When Claudia un-wrapped the wine and saw that it was a red wine, she said, "Oh, I never drink red wine. Here. You can take it back home."

Paolo covered for her by taking the bottle and saying, "Ah, it's a Malbec, my favorite, and I'd be happy if you'd have some with me." Gina responded affirmatively, as did Lydia.

Claudia had ripped the wrapping off the other package, holding it up and saying, "What's this strange thing?"

Gina answered, "It's a wine cork."

I piped in, "And a handsome one, indeed… how pretty."

We were trying to put an end to Claudia's lack of appreciation, but Claudia said, "I won't use it. Take it home, too."

Paolo, Gina, Lydia and I enjoyed conversation throughout dinner. Claudia would occasionally interject something that had nothing to do with the ongoing subject matter. We were hopeful that hearing aids would resolve these kinds of social problems she was having. Lydia and Gina were kind and patient women. We were glad they hadn't abandoned Claudia.

The next day we traveled to the Mission of San Juan Capistrano. Claudia had a potential client who was interested in paintings of it, so she wanted to go there to take photographs that would help her prepare. We hadn't been there before, and it was a beautiful place that we thoroughly enjoyed. The day's bonus was an evening without incident. As we headed on to visit our friends in Laguna and Corona, we felt this visit had gone pretty smoothly.

During the following months a primary subject in Claudia's calls was hearing: hearing tests showing sixty percent hearing loss, hearing aid options, payment plans, return policies. When she finally got her hearing aids, we then were told of too much maddening noise while she was driving, having to hold the phone away from her ear to avoid sound problems from the hearing aids, several rounds of her doctor making sound adjustments to the aids and Claudia's choice not to wear the aids most of the time in order to extend the life of the batteries. The aids were not remedying our problem of having to speak very loudly when we were on the phone with her. She also told us repeatedly that we'd have to speak more slowly, that her doctor had told her that older brains' hearing needed slower vocalizations. Those elements of our phone conversations continued until Paolo finally bought and sent her a new speaker- phone with a portable receiver. After many objections on her part, she finally learned how to operate and adjust it. Though we are sympathetic to anyone suffering hearing loss, Claudia was wearing us out with hers.

She was also sharing and inquiring about details of arrangements she was making to illustrate her friend's book. She also shared details of having her backyard tree taken down and of anonymous notes she was leaving at her neighbor's objecting to their inhumane practice of leaving their dogs out on cold cement in the shade all day. To us, the latter made us caution her about harassment. She assured us that her notes were anonymous and that she wasn't worried.

Of more concern to me was her searching for a way she could afford to go to Zak and Chloe's August wedding in Paris. Claudia had banked enough air miles for roundtrip Europe, so she had Paolo do all sorts of computer research about hotels and car rentals. Hotel rates were beyond her affordability, but as she continued to request car rental rates I wondered if she was considering sleeping in the car. It was heartbreaking for me to know how desperately she wanted to go. I realistically feared she would have to be the center of attention and rob me of the pleasures of the occasion. That quelled my thoughts of giving her the best possible gift of paying for her hotel room. I just couldn't do it. My anxiety was removed when she eventually determined that she couldn't afford it. The wedding weekend in Paris was a storybook experience of pleasures, perfections, and indeed happy memories. We followed it with a pleasure-filled week's cruise on the Siene. The cruise included our first visit to Monet's garden where Claudia had painted several times.

Leftovers

For our birthday trip the next year we started with a few days of visiting friends in Scottsdale, Arizona. From there we planned to spend four nights at Claudia's and three more nights with friends up the coast. Other than telling Claudia that we'd come again for her birthday, we avoided speaking of the pre and post plans to delay her predictable translation that we loved other people more than we loved her. It also put off her predictable assignments of what we "must" see and do in Scottsdale. Though she was knowledgeable about places and often had good suggestions, it was the "assignment" nature of the suggestions that was burdensome. Afterwards, she'd press on whether we'd done the things she suggested. If we hadn't, we got scolded for missing the opportunity.

Claudia's worries for the past several months included the required driver's test she'd have to take before her birthday. The associated eye test worried her the most. Her astigmatism in one eye had worsened her distance vision, a potential cause for her to fail the test. She confessed to cheating on the eye exam four years prior by peeking between her fingers that were supposedly covering her "good" eye in order to read the chart. She didn't want to have to wear glasses for driving. If so, she wanted the glasses to be her favorite heart-shaped sunglasses.

During those months Claudia went to places that offered free eye exams. She paid for eye exams in two other places, but they were unable to craft lenses that would fit into her heart-shaped frames. After encountering every complication that could possibly occur in the process she finally had a pair of prescription glasses made. She tried to memorize eye charts to help her pass the driver's test without glasses. Her plan was that if she failed, she'd then show that she had appropriate glasses for driving. So that she wouldn't have to take the test a second time she'd convince the examiner that her glasses satisfied the requirement.

We advised her to schedule her driver's test early to avoid chancing a period of time restricting her from driving without glasses. She complained about the various DMV locations, the distances, the parking problems, the hours they were open. We also emailed her a National Drivers Test program to help her prepare for the written test. She appreciated that, since it included rules of the road she needed to know. She was also glad that she scheduled her exam early when she learned that most places had a wait of several weeks before they had time slots available. With California's state deficit requiring State workers to take some time off, Claudia was fortunate to get her driver's test taken care of and her license renewed.

During January she was concerned with her dentist's advice that she should have a wisdom tooth removed. Her tooth hadn't bothered her, but her dentist said the removal would be healthier for her other teeth. She scheduled it for after our birthday visit. A greater annoyance and major expense quoted at nine hundred fifty dollars was for removal of two of Celeste's teeth. The poodle supposedly had major gum problems and a tiny tooth with decay. Claudia conveyed every detail of that episode to us including that they hadn't removed any tooth of Celeste's in whatever exorbitantly expensive process they did. They did promise to do a free extraction on her next appointment and reduce the initial fees by several hundred dollars. In the myriad related stories, it was impossible for us to decipher what had or hadn't occurred or at what expense.

When Claudia learned the specifics of our trip, she pressed us to at least arrive a day earlier than our already-booked flight from Phoenix to San Diego. She was very disappointed that we couldn't arrive on Saturday night so that we could all go to her favorite seaside restaurant for its Sunday champagne brunch. Eventually she accepted that we'd be arriving late Sunday afternoon, and she planned an early evening dinner with several friends at her house for us to join. She also told us where she'd like to go for lunch on Monday, and where we'd celebrate her birthday on Tuesday. She was glad we'd be staying with her at least until Thursday. She said she planned to give me a blue cashmere sweater that didn't work well with her wardrobe, so that I'd have something warm for the cool evenings, and that I shouldn't bring boots because she'd give me a pair that no longer fit her.

The week before we commenced our trip Claudia told us that a cover of algae had accumulated in her swimming pool. She was having the pool drained and cleaned. California was about to impose one of its water-restriction programs, so Claudia had hired the drain and clean project to be done before we got there.

Claudia emailed us during our time in Arizona advising that we should shower and wash our hair before we got to her house. Water restriction was in effect and we should plan to flush the toilets only when necessary.

After a delightful three days in Arizona, we headed on to Claudia's. Welcoming hugs and greetings were secondary to her telling us that she couldn't be more miserable. That day she had several problems with her car. Also her bedroom toilet wasn't working. She'd done errands earlier in the day. Lots of smoke from under the hood and a warning sign on her dashboard made her pull over and turn off her car. A fellow who helped her told her to put antifreeze instead of water in the radiator to stop the leak. She also needed more air in one tire, something she hadn't done. And when she got home her toilet seemed to be on perma-flush!

Paolo went immediately upstairs, turned off her toilet, and showed her how to turn it on and off as needed. He learned on the computer that the toilet was an old, discontinued model and parts weren't available.

Claudia came with us as we took our luggage upstairs. She immediately went to our closet, pulled out a pair of black modified western-style boots for me to try on. They did fit me, about which she was happy as she pulled out a pair of tan suede similarly styled boots. They fit, too, as did the third pair, fashionable knee-high black boots that looked brand new except for a tiny spot on one toe that she said I could cover over with a black magic marker. So she wished me a happy birthday. Three pair of boots was indeed a surprise, and I expressed my gratitude.

Getting out the sheets we'd gotten for her last year, she helped me make our bed. We went downstairs where Celeste continued jumping and yapping behind the gates in the family room. Celeste stopped the racket when she was allowed to join us. Claudia showed me the large pot of paella warming on the kitchen stove for that night's dinner. She spoke of how expensive and difficult it was to find the ingredients. She said she'd been working on it for three days though it hadn't turned out like any paella she'd had previously. She said she'd never made it again and hoped it was edible. It looked and smelled wonderful.

She also said that we were probably surprised at how many surfaces she managed to clear in her extensive house cleaning. It was indeed remarkable that the customary stacks of magazines and paperwork, coupons and flyers were out of sight in the dining room. We sat down in the living room where I spotted copies of the new children's book her friend had written, with Claudia as illustrator. I picked up a copy reading it aloud as I complimented her page by page. She said she suspected they wouldn't make any money on it since publishing it cost $5.95 per book. Claudia was glad she'd been paid in advance for the artwork and was given ten copies of the completed book. Claudia was selling them for seven to nine dollars apiece. She thought they cost nine in the bookstore chain where they'd been marketed. I told her I'd be happy to buy seven copies from her. She seemed both surprised and unenthusiastic, asking, "Why would you want so many?"

I answered that I figured seven copies was all I could get in my suitcase and still be within the airline's weight limits. I said that the book was delightful, that people continue to have babies, and that the books made perfect gifts. She seemed somehow annoyed and said she only had four copies left, one of which she had to keep.

I asked if she could get more from the author. I didn't get an answer. She instead asked if I'd noticed how different her backyard looked since she'd taken out the tree. So we went to look at the yard with far more open skies due to the large eucalyptus tree being gone.

"Miguel worked his buns off to get the stump out. He only charged me four hundred, and boy, did he work!"

The guests arrived, a young pleasant couple, he, the fellow who helped her resolve computer-printer problems. Lydia, her realtor, whom we always saw when we visited, arrived shortly thereafter, bringing a batch of her excellent cookies.

The champagne glasses were filled and I helped Claudia serve the bowls of paella that were enthusiastically received and enjoyed. Claudia decided to read us several of her poems about love. Then she said she wasn't the only poet at the table, and she read a copy of a love-poem the printer fellow had written to his wife. He and his wife were surprised by this addition. We complimented his poem. Everyone accepted the offer of another round of paella. The second, or was it the third bottle of champagne, was also enjoyed. As the rest of us conversed, Claudia having chosen not to wear her hearing aids and thereby missing much of the conversation left the table. The guests all had long rides home and full days of work the next day, so it wasn't long before they left. Claudia was there to say good-bye, and then said she was exhausted and went to bed. I cleaned up the dishes and put the leftovers away. We were exhausted, too, and pleased that the evening had gone smoothly.

In the morning Claudia told me what a darling I was to have cleaned up all the dishes and put things away. At breakfast we talked about the timetable for our drive and lunch at the Inn at Rancho Santa Fe and her hopes to find some galleries open in the town. While I took a bath and dressed after breakfast, Claudia went with Paolo to the computer room to look up some information on toilet replacements. I went in and saw stacks of papers on top of the desk, learned that they were her autobiography and got permission to read it. There were multiple copies hither thither, so I spent the first half-hour simply sorting them into sets of ascending page numbers, only two sets complete as far as she'd gotten. During any spare time I could find during the visit I would read it.

I was surprised to find that it started with her winning the Vogue contest just before she graduated from college. I figured that she'd get to accounts of her childhood later. To me, information about formative years is a significant part of an autobiography, incidents of those early years that influenced the shaping of a life. Childhood accounts and references to family members were particularly of interest to me. I read on and on, not finding them.

We had a very scenic ride on this lovely day to the Inn. While in the car I brought up our friends' invitation to visit and lunch with them on Coronado Island of San Diego and asked if we could include it when we visited the zoo. Though Claudia had squelched the idea when I'd mentioned it to her the prior day, she said the hotel dining room there was wonderful, and that we could include it.

We found the Inn's restaurant rustically elegant with an expensive menu. When the waiter came to take our drink order Paolo and I ordered cocktails, and Claudia asked the waiter's suggestion for a white wine, agreeing to his choice. We lunched leisurely, found our meals both delicious and filling, and chose one dessert with three forks to share. When the bill arrived, something that Paolo always checks carefully, he said, "Your glass of wine was twelve dollars."

Claudia responded, "I had no idea." This sufficed for the wine tete-a-tete he and Claudia had.

We walked the half-block across the street into town. It was disappointing that the art center Claudia wanted to visit was closed. Almost everything was closed. We found one tiny gallery next to a floral courtyard open, but Claudia found none of the artworks of quality or interest. Rain started sprinkling so we walked back to the car for the trip home.

Claudia joined me in weeding the gardens that afternoon. In all the past years, my weeding and yard work had been a solo endeavor. She spoke of how she just couldn't keep up with the weeding and was amazed at my energy and speed of accomplishment. She noted a larger plant she wanted out, one I'd bypassed in feeling certain that it wasn't a weed. Her micromanagement took over my systematic process, but eventually she left and I finished the portions I'd planned.

By then Claudia was back in the computer room with Paolo. That gave me time to read more of her autobiography. Once again I noticed the absence of family references, except for her occasional successful pleas for financial assistance from Mom and Dad. There were also several bizarre episodes she reported of throwing one piece of jewelry or another out an apartment window or car window in an unexplained response to something said by whoever she was with. And I was surprised to learn that she had socialized with the famous dancer, Jacques D'Amboise while she was in New York. She'd never mentioned that to me despite my lifelong involvement with dance.

Claudia never asked me what I thought about her autobiography; and I knew I was on safer ground not to comment or ask questions. My reading time was limited, so I was rushing through it. Later I would learn that there were forty or so more pages that I never got to read. Before we left I asked if I could take a copy. Her response, with intense eye-contact was, "Oh, no," as she tick-tocked her finger as if to a child reaching in the cookie jar. I didn't pursue it any farther.

Regarding birthday gifts, though Claudia had requested that she only wanted a check and nothing else, I'd brought along several token gifts. The day we arrived I'd given her a set of handmade plain white paper note-cards and envelopes, and a package of French-design paper dinner napkins.

Her response to the note-cards was, "What is this?" I responded that I thought she might like them for making her own Valentines. For the napkins she simply thanked me.

On her birthday I gave her <u>An Encyclopedia of Roses</u> since they were her favorite flower and she was always investing in new ones. She seemed to appreciate it. In a later chat she said, "I hope Paolo is giving me a nice check for my birthday with all these expenses I'm facing."

I informed her, "No, Paolo doesn't give you checks. Any checks come from me, just like the Christmas check." And I started to worry that she had altered her position that she expected a check equivalent to what we otherwise would have spent on videos she'd requested. A check ten times the fifty dollar amount I'd planned wouldn't have covered the expenses she kept interjecting into conversations.

Continuing with her birthday celebration, we dressed and drove to the French crepes place she had requested. Initially we thought that plan was for an evening dinner, but she chided us for being silly in not remembering it was for lunch. Despite the one and only waitress inadvertently knocking a couple cups off a ledge when we arrived, and having several other breakage experiences while we were there, the waitress remained good-natured and attentive. She and Claudia got into a steady exchange of sharing jokes, so we had a jovial lunch of excellent salads and crepe entrees. We also had excellent samples of several wines before choosing the bottle to accompany lunch. I ate every bite of my entrée. Claudia and Paolo had their leftovers boxed. Once again we shared a dessert that the waitress brought with a little candle in it. As a happy birthday gift to Claudia, as well as an apology for all the clattering mishaps that had surrounded us, that waitress gave us free glasses of a superb dessert wine. We liked it so much that Paolo bought a small bottle for a special eleven dollar price the waitress gave him. Claudia said she'd like a bottle too. The waitress halved the price for her, and Paolo paid the total.

We'd had a good lunch and a fun afternoon before driving back to Carlsbad. At my request we stopped at a resale shop. Claudia protested, and declined my invitation to join me. She stayed in the car while Paolo got out to window shop. Having chosen to wash my hair rather than using water to wash sweaters at Claudia's, I'd found a suitable sweater to tide me through. Back in the car within fifteen minutes, Claudia begrudgingly opened her eyes to look at the sweater I showed her. No comment.

After getting into lounging clothes at home, I gave Claudia an Estee Lauder gift pack of sample products. She unzipped the bag, barely glanced at the contents and said, "Why did you give me this?"

I responded, "Its Estee Lauder. Hers are the products you've often suggested I get. I don't use mascara, so I thought you'd like it and the other samples."

She looked at me and said, "Here's a piece of advice. Never give another lady beauty products. Take it back." As she held it out to me, I took it.

Shortly thereafter she said, "Do you think we can take it to the store and exchange it for some perfume?"

"No. We can't."

"Don't you think they'd exchange it or give you a refund?"

"No. I don't," I replied. "I got it at Boston Store in Milwaukee. You don't have Boston Stores here."

"Well, they have Estee Lauder counters here that should honor it."

"No," I asserted, "We can't take it back. It's all right that you don't want it. I'll take it home." The subject was dropped.

Eventually that evening Paolo and I got hungry. Claudia didn't want anything to eat, so Paolo and I went to the refrigerator where Paolo got out his leftovers. I opened Claudia's leftover box. Most of it was salad getting soggy in its dressing along with about five bites of leftover crepe. That would serve me fine and wouldn't be any good by the next day. I ate it right out of the box.

Claudia came into the kitchen as I was finishing the last bites. Her eyes opened wide and she nearly shouted, "You're eating my leftovers!"

"They're delicious," I said, still in the framework of thinking I was dispensing of them in the last timetable in which they'd be enjoyable.

"You're eating my leftovers!" came again in a convincing tone that I was definitely doing something that wasn't allowed.

To me, that framework was unbelievable. I thought she must be playing with me, so I laughed and said, "They were delicious. If they were still here I'd do it again."

Then I realized that she was furious. "I didn't think you were serious," I said. "I've eaten them. I'm sorry."

She turned to Paolo and said, "Can you believe she just ate my leftovers?"

I couldn't undo what I'd done, nor could I have imagined her eventual plans about the incident.

The next morning was a nice day for our drive into San Diego and Coronado Island. We arrived at Zoe's and Sheldon's home. It was a delightful house and backyard garden full of a huge collection of things from their extensive travels. It was like a mini-museum of masks, carvings, artworks, memorabilia, even a nearly full-sized wonderful wooden horse in their entry hall. The rooms were each painted in different bright colors. The tour was a treat. They also treated us to a fine lunch at the hotel in Coronado Cays. Claudia was their focus of attention during lunch. She'd brought the collection of photos of her artwork. They lauded her exceptional talent. Then she showed them pictures of illustrations from her new children's book. We were dumbfounded that she hadn't brought an actual copy of the book, but Zoe and Sheldon were delighted with the illustrations, and Sheldon told the story of a children's book he'd written but never published.

After lunch they drove us through the area of Coronado Cays, telling us its history and their history there and pointing out various architectural styles in the homes. And as we got back to their house they invited us in to show us the illustrations Sheldon had hired done for his book, and he read us the charming story written in rhyme.

By then we needed to head on to the zoo. Claudia had brought coupons that would take five dollars off each of our entries. Paolo had told me beforehand that he had no interest in going through the zoo again, but he was willing to if necessary.

It was four o'clock when we reached the entrance, and we noted that the zoo was only open until five. We still didn't know who, what, or where Claudia was planning to do her book promotion there. We assumed that she knew. At the admissions window we learned that there was no senior discount, and that the coupons didn't apply. Claudia gave the man her credit card that he processed and said, "That's ninety dollars."

Paolo and I were astounded. Paolo said, "No...thirty dollars apiece for an hour? I'm not going!"

"That's too much," I said to Claudia. "I'll wait here with Paolo."

Claudia said, "I want to see the pandas," and she asked the man the quickest way to get there. She had the first credit card statement destroyed, and bought her ticket. I assured her that we'd meet her exactly in the same place when she was done. Paolo and I waited for the hour, occasionally moving the car closer to the gate until she arrived. Then we learned there was no marketing she could do. They'd told her that the person she needed to see was at the downtown office, which by then was closed. But she had seen the pandas, and thanked us for waiting for her.

At home we had the end of the leftover paella and an uneventful evening. I hurried my way through what I thought was as far as she'd gotten in her autobiography.

The next morning after breakfast, while she and Paolo were in the kitchen I placed my hundred dollar check on the dining room table; and I put the three copies of her new book in my suitcase. I had put my hair up and was putting on my earrings when she came into the bedroom. She said, "Thank you for the check. I have a special gift for you."

She was trying to put a necklace over my head. I balked instinctively, not wanting to do my hair another time. I took the necklace hoping it had a clasp that would allow around-the-neck rather than an over-the-head system. Claudia said she knew how I loved lapis lazuli, and that this necklace was from a dear friend of hers who had died and left Claudia a shoebox full of jewelry. Claudia said the necklace was worth at least a hundred dollars.

The necklace had a screw clasp that had forged itself together. As I was coping with the awkwardness of the situation, Claudia detailed the story of this woman who so lovingly had left her jewelry to Claudia. She kept weaving in the hundred dollar value.

I apologized for not putting the necklace on, explained the problem with my hair, asked if she didn't want to keep the necklace, and thanked her for it.

She went downstairs as I finished packing. She was sitting in the living room when I brought the first suitcase down.

"Oh," I said, "I have the three extra copies of your book in my suitcase."

She immediately said, "You mean that's included in your check?"

"Yes," I said.

She gave me one of her looks and said, "I don't think that's fair."

"How dare you say that?" is what I wanted to bark back at her. But I managed to say nothing. She watched me go to my purse and get out my checkbook.

She said, "They're nine dollars each." She paused briefly and said, "Then there's tax." She paused again and said, "Maybe there's not tax since they're going out of state."

I wrote a thirty dollar check, handed it to her, said nothing and went back upstairs as my adrenalin pumped. My internal rage was about manipulation, power, control, walking on eggs, being gagged, frustration, resentment, emotions, sensibilities, sensitivities, audaciousness, judgment, stupidity, reason, logic, escape, avoidance, expectations, disappointments, history, future, annoyance, aggravation, ad infinitum. Why, just then when we were leaving, had she set up this conflict? What recovery did she expect from me about her assertion that I was unfair? What longer-range plan was she contemplating? My hopes for a pleasant departure were dashed. I simply wanted to get out of there. We couldn't leave fast enough.

Paolo, upstairs packing his suitcase said, "We almost made it without incident this time."

I went back downstairs with my remaining stuff. Claudia with dog in lap was sitting in the corner chair, eyes cast down, nervously twirling her fingers in Celeste's coat.

I said, "Are you still angry?"

She looked at me and said nothing.

Paolo brought down the other suitcase, said "good-bye" and we left.

En route to our next destination, I ranted on to Paolo what I'd held back from Claudia. Thirty dollars, a hundred dollars, whatever, was a ridiculous trigger for my regurgitation of thoughts.

We had a wonderful time with our friends during the remainder of the trip. My mind, however, kept searching for how to bring some suitable resolution with Claudia. On the flight home I drafted a "love and money" letter to her. At home we were surprised to find that no calls from Claudia awaited us on our answering machine.

My letter expressed my sadness that all the pleasurable treks, meals and adventures we'd shared had ended on a sour note, one that was about love and money. Cash values of gifts and conversations about money were subjects that distressed both of us and would be best to leave out of our relationship. I was sorry she was having hearing and hearing aid problems that worried her especially about their effect on marketing her artwork. I was sorry that I had no solutions. The solution I thought best for preserving our relationship was to bypass requests or expectations for money. Serving as a venting board about money matters was something I could no longer do.

I got no response from Claudia. Instead she wrote to Paolo who shared her letter and his response with me. Hers, full of capitalizations and exclamation points, said I'd sent her a very annoyed and annoying letter clearly disallowing her ever again to mention any money concerns. Her letter included dollar-amount details of her toilet repair and her tooth removal, but went on to proclaim that she'd no longer write to him about financial concerns. She assessed that I had two personalities, a sweet helpful one and a trying unnerving one, and that she was saddened that our visit had ended in such a way that it was probably our last. She suggested that he not mention the letter to me to avoid "a *HELLuva Mess!*"

Paolo's response to her explained how upset and hurt I was by various episodes of her behavior. He pointed out that she ignored money-saving advice he'd sent. In so doing, that made his efforts simply a waste of time. He cautioned her to be aware that my side of the story had justification.

A week before my mid-March birthday, I received a commercial birthday card from her, no letter enclosed. I emailed a thank you for it plus the boots and necklace she'd given me when we'd visited. I gave a brief update of our activities, and I encouraged her to invite Zoe and Sheldon to come see her home gallery.

Shortly thereafter Claudia e-mailed a short response stating that it would be best not to plan on celebrating her birthday anymore in Carlsbad since "the last one depressed me greatly!" Rather than signing off with love as she usually did, she signed, "All the Best."

Taking a couple days to think through an ameliorating response I wrote her a review of all the pleasant aspects of our last visit. I also referenced her past expressions of unhappiness that we visited other people rather than spending more time with her. I clarified that what she saw as implication that our enjoyment of them diminished our affection for her wasn't the case. Rather than sustaining the expense of multiple flights to California, we'd always choreographed routes that allowed us to see a number of our California friends in combination with her birthday or at other times we visited. No offense or diminishment of her was involved or intended. We wished she would simply understand that was a practical decision on our part, and not as a comparative value of love or companionship.

Just before I closed my computer that night I found an email response from Claudia entitled "my feelings." Her feelings were that though she appreciated our former help and friendship, our last visit was, in her capital letters, "the *WORST BIRTHDAY OF MY LIFE!!!*" She pointed out that she'd offset the cost of her birthday lunch wine by not ordering dessert, and that she did not find charming that I had later eaten her left-overs. It concluded that birthday parties there were over!

Perhaps a month passed before Claudia resumed calling as if nothing had happened, just as she'd done on former fall-outs. Contents of the calls hadn't changed. My hot-buttons were on alert, and I sensed hers were too. Paolo concurred with my assessment and agreed with my request not to include me when she called. He took the calls. If he wasn't home, I didn't answer. Because she didn't use the speaker-phone Paolo had sent her, nor wear her hearing aids, she would ask Paolo repeatedly to speak more slowly and loudly. Eventually exhausted by that, he told her to stop calling, to just email because the phone had become a futile means of communication. She agreed.

Though she'd banned us from future visits, thereby limiting prospects for our relationship, I encouraged her to email "I'm okay" assurances. Her emails told of eye surgeries, of brief encounters with new people she thought would buy paintings, and of an escalating series of falls. She gashed her arm when she fell in her garage. Waiting for that to heal meant she couldn't swim, thereby eliminating her only exercise. Black eyes and abrasions were the result of two other falls. Then she told us of an incident when on an errand to a government building. An attack of vertigo made her decide to crawl up rather than risk walking up the stairs to the building! That prompted people to call a rescue squad that did blood tests on her. A policeman drove her home. On other occasions police were called by her neighbors who requested they come to help her up when she fell in her driveway while walking back from her street-side mailbox. She enlisted Darlene and Carl to bring the mail to her door and set her trashcans out for collection. She'd accompany some of these reports with, "No, don't plan to visit!"

In response to her increasing financial worries my next email recommended the solution of a reverse-mortgage with an explanation of how it worked. She hated that idea, said she'd NEVER do it, and that she didn't need to hear a word more from me. Emails between the two of us ended.

However, she and Paolo continued to exchange emails for nearly two years. With her reports about weakness and vertigo he cautioned her about driving. We didn't want her to kill or maim herself or innocent others in a car crash. She discounted that worry by telling how people helped her to and from her car at the market and the bank. House-problems, computer-problems and bills were the content of her emails until she focused on a "Save the Wild Horses" organization's campaign. She pressed Paolo to donate to it and to enlist all his friends to do the same. He responded that he thought the government policy on reducing the herd was more humane than letting the increasing number of wild horses starve to death. Infuriated, she responded that his position proved him to be a cruel, unloving man and that she would have no more to do with him.

Shortly thereafter we learned that she emailed Zak, cast aspersions on Paolo as untrustworthy, and directed that Zak look into my financial affairs to assess if Paolo was taking advantage of me. By that, Paolo was enraged and wanted to sue her for slander. She had gone too far. Only at my repeated request did he not activate the suit. Paolo erased her email from his list.

Lydia's was the only contact number we had, and even she didn't know Darlene's last name or phone number. After the Thanksgiving incident at Lydia's when inebriated Claudia choked on a bite of turkey and they took her to the emergency room against Claudia's wishes, Claudia told Lydia never to call her again. As far as we knew Claudia had also removed my name as the person to contact in case of emergency.

The only tie Claudia hadn't severed was with Zak. For seven more months we received his accounts of cards, little gifts to his kids, brief updates and Claudia's ear surgery. Between those reports we didn't know if she was dead or alive.

In May Paolo noticed that Claudia started a Facebook account on which she stated that she'd moved. We asked Zak to ask her about it. A few days later I received an email from Claudia that stated with annoyance that she definitely hadn't moved but was simply learning how to use Facebook. A month later I received another "wild horses" email obviously as part of her whole mailing list, once again stating her support and enlisting everyone else and their friends to donate. It, as almost any reference to Claudia, prompted many negative reflections. I reflected on how often and easily I'd taken the bait of her manipulations. It boiled down to "stupid me." I thought Mother had probably reached the humiliation of "stupid me" when in late life she wrote to Claudia that she had a number of "favorite charities" to which she donated instead of perpetually sending money to Claudia. Claudia had raged to me about it and was further enraged when I had declined her request to write to Mother about the greater importance of helping family members than supporting charities. That was reminiscent of Claudia pushing for my being the messenger to our dying Aunt Priscilla so many years ago. The twist on that appeal was that Priscilla should maintain dedication to her blood relatives rather than to the recent strangers who'd endeared themselves to her just for the money. When Priscilla died, "the vultures" as Claudia called them, managed to inherit Priscilla's three-quarter of a million estate.

Claudia's pulling the plug on family and saying she planned to leave her estate to the wild horses clearly belied her former stances. Each revelation of Claudia's final decisions spurred my sadness of how her intelligence, talents, and attributes had succumbed to alcohol. Though she could succeed in hiding it for a few hours with new people she met, she had become a pathetic drunk. It also made me wonder about what base or innocent elements of my own character I'd failed to acknowledge and discipline. Like a wild horse in survival mode, how many times had I taken the carrots of temptation she held out to me? If I outlived her and if she hadn't used up her estate or willed it away to some incidental recipient or charity, I had delightful fantasies about how I'd undo the damages she'd inflicted on family and friends. I imagined having gatherings of our kids and grandkids at her house, the kids swimming in her pool, all of us sharing meal preparations and taking jaunts to the inviting activities of the San Diego area. I imagined setting up a schedule of times for our nieces and nephews to use the house with their families. Escapes from Wisconsin winters and having our California friends and other friends come visit us in Carlsbad were among my fantasies. That carrot was huge and particularly tasty. These fantasies were hard to abandon no matter how remote their likelihood.

Mystery/Ashes/Insights

In late October, awakened near midnight from a sound sleep, we groggily answered the phone. It took a moment to realize the call was from the Medical Examiner's office in San Diego notifying us that Claudia was dead. Her neighbors, noticing that the mail they'd left on her door was still there two days later, called the police. The police and homicide squad used Darlene's key to enter where they found Claudia's body in the downstairs hallway. They followed procedure of having the medical examiner come to observe the scene, pronounce her dead, take the body and call next-of-kin. We answered some questions of medical history in the family and our knowledge that she wished to be cremated with her ashes thrown into the sea. They requested that we get back to them to make further arrangements for the body and contacts for her estate. We learned that Darlene was allowed to take the dog, and they gave us Darlene's number.

We decided it was wiser to try to go back to sleep and to discuss it in the morning.

At breakfast the next day, though Paolo said just to pack up and go out there, I needed time to look through my several bulging files on Claudia, hoping that I'd find her attorney's numbers or other contact numbers that might help us. Numerous changes and notifications would need to be made. If we did go we'd also have to cancel and rebook all sorts of things on our calendar in addition to notifying my kids and relatives. How long would we need to be out there? What papers, documents, or information would we have to take?

Zak advised that we needed to learn who the executor or trustee was before we went to Carlsbad. If we weren't named as such, we could be sued for illegally entering the house, and assertions could be made that things were no longer there that were there before we entered! I managed to find the scrap of paper with Claudia's initial attorney's contact info. In the meanwhile California's Public Administration office called us to say they hadn't found a will at the premises and needed it in order to proceed.

Lydia called, shocked at the news, but saying that Claudia had given her a copy of the will. She'd FAX it to us. She also said that she and her husband had recommended a local attorney friend of theirs to ease Claudia's concerns that her original attorney was too great a distance away.

In my call to the initial attorney she too was shocked and sorry for our loss. She said she was looking at a beautiful painting Claudia had given her, that Claudia was "quirky" but a fine artist and poet. Answering my question of whether she had Claudia's Neptune Society cremation membership, she said no, but advised that it was worth getting comparative costs from a dozen funeral homes to dodge the outrageous thousand dollars some of the hustlers charged. The attorney had the trust and will and the amendment that listed us as executors and trustees after Claudia had eliminated Clarke from any benefits. But then the attorney found a later amendment that listed Lydia as executor and beneficiary with ten thousand left to me and five thousand to my younger nephew who was also listed as beneficiary of her State Teachers retirement fund. Those were the only other designations.

That prompted me to convey that unfortunately Claudia had taken the dive into alcoholism, drank a magnum of wine daily, started earlier and earlier in the day, was slurringly drunk by late afternoon, and staggeringly drunk by early evening, sometimes falling. The attorney responded that contesting the will was an unlikely win. Claudia exhibited no stupor or intoxication during their conversations or on the call requesting the amendment. The amendment was written per Claudia's directions. Then it was mailed to Claudia who signed and returned it promptly. The attorney said that alcohol didn't factor into Claudia's legal arrangements.

Paolo and I found it strange that Lydia hadn't mentioned that she was primary inheritor of Claudia's estate. Perhaps she'd gotten the will before this particular amendment had been made to it.

We also reached Darlene who told us that Claudia had probably been dead for two days before being found. Homicide had taken a lot of photos particularly in the dining room and the stairwell and had come back to take more. She had no idea what the homicide squad might be pursuing. She gave us the contact number of the police officer who took her copy of Claudia's contact list, and then wouldn't give it back. The dog was now in another neighbor's care, a long-ago prearranged plan. Darlene repeated the mail story, calling the police and getting Princess. Upon seeing the situation the policeman said to her, "I'm sorry. She's gone. Things seem peculiar."

Darlene told the forensics team that Claudia was a "very eccentric lady who enjoyed her chardonnay. It isn't peculiar she was found in little clothing." We later learned that Claudia was wearing her jeans, nothing on top when she was found.

Darlene also told us of her discomfort about a year ago when Claudia introduced her to "a Dan", and said in his presence, "This is who will inherit everything of mine."

Darlene tried to take Claudia aside. When Darlene said, "Do you trust him?" Claudia made a straight-arm, stay back gesture to Darlene, and said, "We're not talking about it."

The night Claudia was found Darlene asked the police if they knew of a man who visited Claudia. The policeman said, "Dan?" but nothing more was said. Darlene told us that Dan's blue car was usually at Claudia's once or twice a month, but they hadn't seen it at least for the last two weeks. Darlene added, perhaps because she thought Dan was "the pool guy," that the neighbors had called the State to put mosquito-eating fish in Claudia's pool that was black with muck. Darlene didn't sense a bond in Dan and Claudia's relationship. She didn't sense that he had Claudia's best interest at heart. They never saw him do caretaking like bringing her groceries or driving her on errands. Darlene thought a background check should be done on him.

The homicide information disconcerted us. Good grief! Was murder a potential factor in Claudia's death? Had there also been a robbery? Was there indication of assault or rape? These weren't comforting speculations. It wasn't until a week later that we learned that a homicide investigation is standard practice when a person living alone is found dead. In such cases they automatically investigate the possibility of foul play.

Three days later, Cheri, Princesses inheritor, called us. After pleasantly describing her relationship with Claudia, she said she had a health power-of-attorney, a copy of the will and trust and an amendment dated more recently than the ones we knew of. She said she would send them immediately to us. She said these documents indicated ten thousand to me, five thousand to Paolo and the remainder of the estate to Dan Glover. She didn't know who Dan was other than some scribbled note by Claudia indicating that he was the "pool guy." She said she knew how much we'd done for Claudia over the years on our visits and was sorry Claudia had become so vengeful. I got the new attorney's contact info from her and a phone number for Dan. Cheri said to feel free to call her if we felt there was any more she could do or in case we considered contesting the will. She said she'd go over to the house to see if she could discern anything more.

Our call to the new attorney was mystifying. The secretary who was signed as a witness on the documents was surprised to learn of Claudia's death. She spoke of what an exceptional, talented artist and poet she was. Claudia had given their office some beautiful paintings too. While we waited for the attorney, the secretary brought the file to her desk. We waited longer. She eventually said, "Let me see the file and whether we can even talk to you." That was an unexpected and shocking statement. I asked what she meant as I reasserted that I was Claudia's sister, the only remaining member of her family of origin, that we needed to know what the documents designated and whether they also had a copy of Claudia's Neptune membership so that we could proceed with her wish to be cremated. The secretary said her boss was still on his call but that she'd have him call us back.

On the fourth day postmortem Cheri reported that while she was meeting impromptu with Darlene and Carl, Dan pulled up. He came across the street to introduce himself to them. He said he was going to the house to get some things the lawyer had directed him to do. They told him the house was sealed meaning no one should enter. Cheri asked if he was the "pool guy," and he avowed he wasn't, that the pool was in terrible condition and the pool guy was worthless. Dan said, "I'm not the pool guy, just friends for three years." Dan then went to the house, was in for about five minutes and came out empty-handed.

Cheri asked if I knew anything about an oil lease Claudia had. I told her that over thirty of us as relatives of a long-deceased uncle had mineral rights in a California property. Cheri said she'd been with Claudia when the lease-renewal piece of mail arrived. Claudia wrote "refused" all over it and returned it. Cheri also said that Claudia had fallings-out with all her doctors and that the eye-doctor, who was also

Cheri's, had deposited two thousand dollars with Claudia two years ago for two paintings Claudia never delivered.

Cheri called again later that day giving us contact information for a highly respected Carlsbad estate attorney she knew. He was willing to do a free consultancy by phone about our prospects of contesting the will. Our brother-in-law had suggested we do that. The referred attorney proved to be in court all day, but would call us Friday.

On Friday I left a message on the answering machine of Claudia's local attorney, and received no call back. The potential "contest" attorney didn't call either. Instead California's Public Administration office called us. I gave them the contact info for the attorney who had the latest documents. Finally his office secretary called us back. Since they were electronically sending Claudia's papers to the public administrator they would also e-mail them to us. She confirmed Dan as the executor-trustee and simply defined him as Claudia's friend for many years.

When the documents arrived they listed Dan as executor, trustee and sole inheritor of Claudia's estate. Claudia had established the last amendment just a month before she died. Dan's wife was listed as successor trustee if Dan predeceased her or refused to serve. Cheri was the next successor if the others refused and/or predeceased her.

After finally consulting with Cheri's recommended attorney on Monday, the bottom-line was that we could spend twenty to forty thousand dollars to contest the will, but having no direct witness reports of Dan and Claudia's relationship, we would lose. There were no malpractice records on file for the document's attorney and he was held in high esteem by his peers. Making a post-mortem claim of Claudia's incompetence held few prospects, and "undue influence" was impossible without witnesses. The documents would stand.

When we asked about the pros and cons of calling Dan directly we were advised that was a perfectly acceptable thing to do. Considering what to say in such a call was no easy task. My nephew's wife, Kelly, called to let us know that she was vacationing in San Diego that week. She said to let her know if there was anything she could do regarding Claudia's estate while she was there. Kelly was among other relatives and friends who knew our history with Claudia and who had experienced episodes of it themselves. They expressed sympathy and regret for Claudia's lack of appreciation and reward. They also asked about "this guy." What was his relationship with her? What entitled him to inherit her estate? What had he done for her that could possibly have outweighed what we had done? Was he a clever scoundrel? Was he a "prey on the elderly" opportunist? Our curiosity was equally piqued. We additionally wondered about his relationship with the lawyer. Another perplexing curiosity was that the lawyer who had been recommended to Claudia by Lydia and her husband hadn't recused himself when he saw that the changes removed Lydia as major inheritor. It seemed strange that the lawyer getting a new client from a friend would draw up documents that so negatively impacted his friend. Though a lawyer's job is to represent his client to the best of his ability, to carry out his client's wishes within the limits of the law, were there other subjective factors involved in this case? How would we ever know?

On the other hand, what if you developed a mutually cherished friendship with an elderly, childless, single, educated, intelligent, charming person who showed you the documents designating you as beneficiary of her entire substantial estate? Suppose you were also aware that she was an alcoholic, could no longer hear well, walk steadily, manage upkeep on her property, and showed other indicators of age and declining health. Suppose you were uncomfortable about her plans and discussed with her that she had significant relatives and friends to consider. Suppose she convinced you that her family and friends had subjected her to endless unkindness, didn't care about her, and that she owed them nothing. Answers naturally varied among the friends we polled.

The coroner called. We confirmed his speculation that Claudia was a long-established alcoholic. His report indicated that there were no punctures or signs of foul play. He hoped we wouldn't be offended by the question but as a matter of course he asked if we thought she might have committed suicide. We answered that we thought that unlikely and asked that if she had done so, by what means? He answered, "Pills."

We said that to our knowledge she took no prescriptions or medications and was a naturalist well-versed on the healing elements of fruits, vegetable, teas, et cetera.

He went on to tell us that she had acute pancreatitis and an abnormal liver with extensive fatty content, common in chronic alcoholics. She couldn't have felt well, probably not drinking much nor interested in having a glass of wine. Pancreatic enzymes into her bloodstream would have caused a systemic problem. The toxicology reports would take another four to six weeks for final analysis.

Paolo asked if there were any signs of sexual activity. The doctor hadn't examined for that. Though we'd provided the executor's contact information, Claudia's remains were still at the morgue.

Previously concerned about Claudia's museum-quality artworks, and worried that Dan unaware of value might put them in a rummage sale, I continued trying to reach the museum curator. Eventually I learned that the curator we'd met was no longer there. The new curator would look for the records and contact Dan. That provided me a starting point for talking to Dan.

Paolo and I took courage and called Dan. Wondering if caller I.D. might dissuade him from answering we were surprised that he answered quickly. I introduced myself as Claudia's sister and immediately embarked on knowing that Claudia wanted the museum-quality items to be in the San Diego Art Museum to be appreciated by the public. Dan acknowledged that Claudia had educated him about the Buddhas and made a detailed list for him. He said she'd familiarized him with the values of many things in the house.

I blurted in, "Since we've never met you..." and he interrupted, "We met each other ten years ago at a birthday party dinner at Claudia's. Claudia read the love poem that I'd written to my wife." That surged into my memory, and it coupled with chagrin that I'd told everyone that we'd never met "the guy." Paolo didn't remember the event, and neither of us could coax out any visual recollection of Dan or his wife. Dan went on that we all had plenty to drink that evening and a lot of fun. Claudia gave him one of her poetry books as they were leaving. He'd never written a poem before, but with Claudia's appreciation and encouragement poetry was a bond between them. He said that printer-repairs were his business. He had seen Claudia every week or two when she called him for that, although he hadn't seen her since mid-September when he drove her to her attorney appointment. We asked about her health, whether she was sick then. "She seemed fine," he said, "no indications of being physically ill." He hadn't seen her since then because he was housebound after having a surgical procedure.

We told him the pathologist's report of pancreatitis and liver disease common in chronic alcoholics. Dan concurred that "she usually drank too much, but we all do sometimes." He said he needed my okay or

Cheri's to proceed with the cremation. Claudia did leave him a contact name for a cremation quote of seven hundred dollars. Dan continued that he'd never been an executor of an estate before and felt nervous about it. He was meeting with the lawyer later that day for further guidance. He'd found a safety deposit box key but hadn't gone to the bank to find out what documents were there. He'd look for the Neptune Society papers. He said he'd be more than happy for us to take what we particularly liked of her artwork, "after all you're her sister. She left you some money too." Obviously he didn't know that the last copy of her Trust cut us out altogether. He had to leave then for his appointment but said he'd stay in touch.

As spurned relatives in the situation we were cautious in the conversation, consciously squelching all sorts of questions we wanted to ask. Dan seemed open and unaware of what a fortune was his, and of what the documents said. Another discomfort to us was how to respond to Dan's offer of artworks. Paolo couldn't think of one of Claudia's hundreds of paintings that he wanted. I knew clearly a particular one I'd always wanted. Actually I would have liked all of Claudia's sculptures, not to keep but to save for my grandchildren and to give as gifts to relatives and friends. I could imagine that asking for too much could easily cause Dan to squelch the offer. I thereby chose only three things. Upon emailing my list, Dan's reply asked if I wouldn't like to have one of Claudia's sculptures. I added one to my list.

Recalling that Kelly and my nephew had wanted some of Claudia's paintings in that long-ago visit when Claudia made price-negotiation impossible, I asked Kelly to go to Claudia's to give us a report of her observations. She did, with the result of Dan letting her take her favorite painting plus small ones for each of her daughters. She was delighted. At the same time she was repulsed by the filthy disorganized condition of the house and the horrid condition of the pool and grounds. Even thinking of it made her nauseous. She also said Dan's wife, Bonnie, was there and described her as a tiny, cheerful redhead. Even that spurred no visual memories for us. Kelly said that other people were coming and going from the house. She overheard Bonnie and Dan planning to unload all of Claudia's clothing to the Goodwill. Were Claudia's exceptional collection of jewelry and her ermine coat going to the Goodwill too?

Dan emailed, reporting that he was out-of-pocket on Claudia's taxes and bills since the bank would give no access without Claudia's death certificate that was still pending. He said his attorney was sending me fifteen thousand dollars-worth of bonds that had been found listing me as secondary owner. I silently recalled the unpleasant episode with Claudia about the H-bonds from Mother's estate.

Nearly three weeks passed before the bonds arrived. It took an hour and a half with my banker to begin the complex process on the bonds that would take another three weeks for the funds to be transferred into my account. As it turned out, the Treasury Department didn't have answers about the bonds until after year's end. The answers were that a decade ago Claudia had reported the bonds lost, had them reissued and redeemed them for full value in the years they matured. That was that.

As our boxes of acquired possessions arrived, we saw that Dan had generously included five more of Claudia's sculptures. We felt nothing maudlin or sad in finding suitable places for everything. As opposed to painful memories, we simply enjoyed Claudia's artworks as attractive artworks.

For me the most painful memories included Claudia's treatment of my Mother, my sons and of Paolo. I had assessed after Claudia's death that I could have spared them their experiences of hurt and anguish. Claudia's early declaration of being a "Spirit" was a masterful manipulation insinuating Divine rather than Satanic. In retrospect, such manipulations are obvious and manageable. By betraying my own sense of integrity, and too often bypassing constructive candor in communicating with Claudia, I'd allowed a damaging and demeaning relationship to prevail. Instead of exposing and helping her understand the hurt and injuries others suffered from her statements and actions and the deception of her self-image of being spiritual, kind-hearted and uplifting, I'd failed to enforce reasonable boundaries for any of us. Such efforts probably wouldn't have met with success, but a result of severance would have spared all of us decades of painful futility. I apologized to my family.

Though Ahab stories are intriguing, there is pleasure in more positive "you're not going to believe this" stories that are celebrations of achievement, prevailing when the odds are fiercely against you, overcoming handicaps, surviving health problems, or having something wonderful happen when you least expect it.

A few days after we received the news of Claudia's death, over eight hundred Trick-or-Treaters reaped the rewards of our pear harvest. Despite our urban setting, a group of wild turkeys settled in our neighborhood until the winter depths of snow and sub-zero temperatures took over. Under the snow we knew the flowers would burst forth in spring.

POSTSCRIPT

From Incite to Insight or Vice Versa

There are many sayings that pop into mind when you have problems:

"Do unto others...
Get it off your chest.
Tell it like it is.
If at first you don't succeed..."

Heeding these messages sometimes helps to prompt constructive candor with our family, friends and society. Sometimes that works; sometimes it doesn't.

There are dozens more sayings of a different ilk:

"Let a sleeping dog lie.
Silence is golden.
No point in talking to a brick wall."

Abiding by these sayings may be wise at times but may unintentionally become collusion, enabling or escape/avoidance serving to perpetuate the problem.

In sharing stories about difficult family members, situations or episodes from others that begin with, "You're not going to believe this," you learn how many common grounds you share. It's a relief to know you're not alone in your experiences. It's heartening when others' stories lead you to solutions and closure.

Forthright and trusting communication is a gift toward educated understanding. Asking questions and expressing viewpoints that apply to difficult circumstances are fruitful endeavors despite the lack of ease or comfort that often accompany them. It begins with you and your relationships on every level.